the secret blog of

Raisin Rodriguez

the secret blog of

Raisin Rodriguez

a novel by

Judy Goldschmidt

razOr
bill

The Secret Blog of Raisin Rodriguez

RAZORBILL

Published by the Penguin Group
Penguin Young Readers Group
345 Hudson Street, New York, New York 10014, U.S.A.
Penguin Group (USA) Inc., 375 Hudson Street, New York, New York 10014, U.S.A
Penguin Books Canada Ltd, 10 Alcorn Avenue, Toronto, Ontario,
Canada M4V 3B2 (a division of Pearson Penguin Canada, Inc.)
Penguin Books Ltd, 80 Strand, London WC2R 0RL, England
Penguin Ireland, 25 St Stephen's Green, Dublin 2, Ireland
(a division of Penguin Books Ltd)
Penguin Group (Australia), 250 Camberwell Road, Camberwell,
Victoria 3124, Australia (a division of Pearson Australia Group Pty Ltd)
Penguin Books India Pvt Ltd, 11 Community Centre, Panchsheel Park,
 New Delhi – 110 017, India
Penguin Group (NZ), Cnr Airborne and Rosedale Roads, Albany,
Auckland 1310, New Zealand (a division of Pearson New Zealand Ltd)
Penguin Books (South Africa) (Pty) Ltd, 24 Sturdee Avenue,
Rosebank, Johannesburg 2196, South Africa

Penguin Books Ltd, Registered Offices: 80 Strand,
London WC2R 0RL, England

10 9 8 7 6 5 4 3 2 1

ALLOYENTERTAINMENT   Produced by Alloy Entertainment
151 West 26th Street
New York, NY 10001

Library of Congress Cataloging-in-Publication Data

Goldschmidt, Judy.
  The secret blog of Raisin Rodriguez / by Judy Goldschmidt.
    p. cm.
  Summary: In a weblog she sends to her best friends back in Berkeley, seventh-grader Raisin
Rodriguez chronicles her successes and her more frequent humiliating failures as she attempts
to make friends at her new Philadelphia school.
  ISBN 1-59514-018-2 (hardcover)
  [1. Weblogs—Fiction. 2. Interpersonal relations—Fiction. 3. Middle schools—Fiction.
4. Schools—Fiction. 5. Humorous stories.] I. Title.
  PZ7.G574Se 2005
  [Fic]—dc22

                                                            2004018361

Printed in the United States of America

Acknowledgments

Huge thanks to Liesa Abrams, whose creative mind, clarity of thought, dedication, and willingness to take calls on the weekend made this all possible. And to Eloise Flood, who believed in me before I did. Big thanks to Margaret Wright too!

Big big thanks to Leslie Morgenstein, Josh Bank, Ben Schrank, Lynn Weingarten, Lisa Rounds, Chris Grassi, and everyone at the office for their unending support.

To Keith Summa, Maura Tierney, Andy Blackman, and Susan Buttenwieser for all their help.

And to Kelly Kimball and Janine Ditulio, whose limitless generosity kept me sane throughout.

To my family, with love.

Sunday, September 12

Dear Pia and Claudia,

Welcome to TwoScoopsofRaisin.com. Aka my blog. I know there are many blogs out there to choose from. Your choice to read mine is much appreciated.

Why keep a blog? you ask.

Excellent question, I answer.

There are many reasons to keep a blog. Here are just a few I've come up with:

1. You just moved to Philadelphia—far, far away from your two best friends in the world, and you need a way to keep in touch.

2. You'd prefer using the phone, but your new stepsister is constantly hogging it. (Though it's a mystery who she's talking to. She doesn't seem to have a lot of friends.)

3. You'd prefer using the phone, but you were born without a tongue.

   Or

4. You like the word *blog* because it sounds funny.

All of these are good reasons. No one reason is better than another. It just so happens that in my case, reasons one and two apply. Someone else might find reason four to be the most fitting. Another person might recognize him or herself in reason three. If you are that person, I suggest seeking the help of a health-care professional.

I hope you enjoy my blog. Feel free to check for new updates as often as you like. Please do not feel free, under any circumstances, on pain of death, to give the address of this blog to anyone. This blog is very personal and confidential and deals with mature subject matter.

Additionally, unauthorized reading could potentially result in harmful side effects such as eye twitching, sudden memory loss, dry mouth, and butt acne.

Thank you for flying Raisin.

Monday, September 13

4:07 PM, EST

Hello Kitties,

Today I made out with my earth science book. Well, not the book so much as the boy on the cover of the book. We met this morning during seventh-grade orientation at Franklin Academy. Turns out there are more social opportunities at my new school than I had imagined. . . . It's just a matter of knowing where to look.

Which in this case was right in front of my face.

After orientation, I was sitting at my kitchen table, putting covers on all my textbooks like we're supposed to. But when it came time to cover him up, I didn't have the heart to do it. He looked so irresistible, with his hair all floppy and his teeth all gleaming white. And his eyes! They were practically shouting out to the world, "Kiss me, I'm stuck on this book cover." So I laid one on him. I couldn't help myself, really. It was bigger than the both of us. I must say, though, for a piece of cardboard he's quite the kisser. . . .

Sometimes there's just no explaining what goes on between a man and a woman.

Go ahead. Call me crazy. But don't forget, I've been through a lot lately.

Let's review:

1. I was minding my own business, happily living in Berkeley, when my mom and dad decided to get a divorce.
2. My mother invented Ice Dogs (the frozen treats for dogs).
3. Horace bought the company from her.
4. They fell in love and decided to get married.
5. My mother moved to Philly to be with him and brought me (and Lola) along with her.
6. You guys, who I love and depend on (especially for preventing me from doing weird things like kissing boys on book covers), had to stay in Berkeley.
7. And here I am, all by my lonesome.

So I can't really be held responsible for my actions in my present state of mind. (If anyone should be held responsible, it's probably my mother, no?) Especially now that I've discovered a new bad side effect to moving: STARTING OVER IN A NEW SCHOOLLFHGFHfoocooao93]. 'IURFrURLKFJLK dhkhv ;h '/9u vvguv;v xihclipopup9UhgHIOXUJIIFU;Oi./J/qo

SORRY! That was Lola. She loves to pound on my keyboard and say, "I'm doing my work." It makes her feel important. As if speaking those four words will get everyone wondering what brilliant scientific discoveries she's making and forgeting that she's still in Pull-Ups. And I begged my mother to leave her behind when weTTTTTT Gvkjfha;fh;ffj p f f;kKHO IHOIIHOIHOIHOIHOIHOPDIw pjdl kjkjlkjoioijo;ijjhkjhgffdfd diii9999999Jeez Louise! With all the fancy computers around here, I don't know why she has to choose my laptop. I think she just likes being on my bed. Maybe it's the purple velvet comforter. Or the fact that there aren't any safety guards . . .

I suppose I should put in a DVD for her or something. Why must I take care of a toddler on the eve of my first official day of classes? Isn't that the responsibility of my mom and stepdad? I know they have a business to run, but I've got a big day tomorrow.

I should be lounging in a bubble bath. Sipping some chamomile tea. Connecting with my higher power. Or at least watching E! Entertainment Television in order to prepare myself with some intelligent conversation starters.

Ugh, I better go, she won't stop licking my arm.

5:17 PM, EST

I put Lola in front of *Finding Nemo.* But I've only got a couple of minutes before I need to get back to her. Every time that gimpy fish gets chased by the sharks, she gets scared and cries her head off.

So where was I? Oh, right, my new school . . .

I'm not sure I'm going to like this Franklin Academy. Not sure at all . . .

For starters, the decor is very gloomy—all poop brown and farty green. (I know farts have no color, but if they did, this would be it.) And the furniture looks very old-fashioned and stuffy. Like someone will yell at you if you try to sit on it. And the lockers are indoors. Indoors, I tell you! What a scam! Plus no one tried to make me feel welcome in any way. I was expecting *someone* of the adult persuasion to say something like, "Hello, Raisin, we heard your tragic story, and let us just say, it's an honor to have you here." Or at least, "Here's a cookie. . . ."

But nothing.

Made me appreciate the lush setting at Berkeley Middle School. The outdoor lockers built amid the rolling green hills. The comfort of the warm blue carpets. And even the Orientation Day Magic Circle, where

we joined hands to meditate on our hopes for the coming year. Sure, that was pretty corny. And sure, after it
was over, I couldn't look either of you guys in the eye
for days. But I will say one thing. At least we got to
have tea and granola bars afterward. At Franklin
Academy, it's all business. They just sent us straight to
the auditorium to pick up schedules and locker numbers and then off to the book room to pick up books.

Actually, come to think of it, the book room wasn't
so bad. That's where someone actually talked to me. A
guy. He just came charging at me from behind,
grabbed me by the shoulders, and flipped me around.

"Hey, cuteness," he said, looking me up and down
with his piercing blue eyes. "I'm Sparkles. Who are you?"

I wondered if he was that friendly with every
stranger he came in contact with.

"Raisin."

"Greaaaaat name. Mind if I call you New Girl?"

"Sure," I said. He was so hot, he could have called
me Fred for all I cared.

Then he picked up a strand of my hair. "Your high-
lights look faaabulous. Are they from the sun or the
bottle?" That's when it sank in. The clothes (his T-shirt
had a fur collar), the haircut (a bowl, cut exactly the
same as mine), the way he moved (with a lot of attitude, almost like he was dancing). Sparkles wasn't

interested in me for my bootyliciousness, he was interested in me for my beauty tips . . . if you get my drift.

"Neither," I told him. "They don't say it on the box, but Crest White Strips work on hair too."

"New Girl, no way. I must stop at Target on the way home and get myself a box." He gave *Target* a French pronunciation—"Tar-jay."

I was disappointed that Sparkles and I wouldn't be walking off into the sunset together, but talking to him wasn't a complete waste of my time. For one thing, he's an eighth-grader. So maybe he can kind of show me the ropes. Plus he told me that apple vinegar is great for beating the frizzies. And as we all know, I'm always looking for a good frizzies beater.

Ugh! There goes Lola. I better go before she hyperventilates.

5:31 PM, EST

Instead of watching *Nemo* again, Lola asked me to put on the local news. She's a big fan of the weatherman here. Sometimes he wears a giant yellow rain hat and slicker. She thinks it's the funniest thing she's ever seen.

Ooh . . . I just heard my stepsister, Samantha, walk through the door. She's taking Lola and me out to dinner because Mom's working late.

Again.

It's nice to have a mother who's so concerned over the snacking needs of her canine customers, but what about her daughters? I wonder if it ever occurs to her that we could also use a home-cooked treat every once in a while? Or that if she was planning on seeing us so little anyway, she might have considered leaving us in Berkley with my dad.

Or at least *me*. I know they say young children need to be with their mothers. But when you think about it, I'm not the one who's young. It's Lola. She's only four. I'm already twelve going on thirteen.

8:02 PM, EST

Just got back from dinner with Samantha . . . hoagies. You know what a hoagie is? A Philadelphian submarine sandwich. You know why it's called a hoagie?

Me neither.

And neither does Ms. Smarty-Pants Samantha.

After we sat down for dinner, I asked her about it.

"Samantha," I said. "Why do they call it a hoagie here when everyone else calls it a submarine sandwich?"

"I don't know, Raisin," she answered as she put one tiny perfectly rounded potato chip in her mouth.

"Could *hoagie* mean 'submarine sandwich' in a different language or something like that?"

"I don't really know . . ." she answered, still working on that same tiny chip.

For a sophomore taking only Advanced Placement courses, she didn't seem to know much. Either that, or she didn't find the topic of sandwiches intelligent enough to discuss.

That's fine. Two can play at that game. On the walk home, I didn't talk to her at all. I did still look at her, however. Sometimes, I just can't resist. She's the kind of girl who's really pretty even thought she ties her beautiful blond hair all the way back in a ponytail and covers her face with thick ugly grandpa glasses.

She didn't return the favor, though. She was too busy checking her cell-phone messages. It's hard to imagine who's calling her; I never see her with friends. Maybe she belongs to a circle of brainiacs who just leave super-smart messages on each other's cell phones, like "I've isolated the gene for chicken pox in cattle, call me!" or "Sorry I couldn't pick up before, I was moments away from solving world peace."

PS—I've been thinking about the word *embarrassing*. Do you think it comes from the root words *bare* and *ass?*"

PPS—You know how they tell you to break open a vitamin A and spread it on your imperfections? I highly disrecommend it—I tried it last night, and now I smell like cod.

Comments:

Logged in at 7:10 PM, EST

kweenclaudia: can we go back to you kissing the textbook? sounds really romantic. what's next, playing 7 minutes in heaven with a calculator? going out on a date with a loose-leaf?

ps—you're ok with us adding our comments, right? it's really half the fun, dontcha think?

Logged in at 7:12 PM, EST

PiaBallerina: Don't worry, Raisin, Claudia doesn't mean to be nasty about you and the textbook. She just can't help herself sometimes. I hope you don't mind that we're adding our comments . . . miss you!

Tuesday, September 14

7:38 AM, EST

Good morning, Kitties,

After careful consideration, I have decided to permit you two to continue adding your comments to my Web log. But please do keep in mind that this is my sacred and special place.

Off to my first real day of school. It should be much better than yesterday. At least that's what my mother told me.

Wish me luck!

PS—Miss you guys too!

PPS—Though some more than others . . .

PPSS—I'm wearing my gold metallic thong for good luck. I hope you guys are wearing yours!

4:15 PM, EST

Life is full of little lessons. For example, today I learned that sometimes when mothers say things like, "Today will be better than yesterday," they don't necessarily know what they're talking about.

But you know what? I'd rather not discuss it.

4:27 PM, EST

One more lesson: Just because you call a pair of underwear your "good luck" underwear doesn't mean it actually will bring you luck, no matter how shiny it is.

But again, I'm really not in the mood to go into it.

4:43 PM, EST

I said I'd prefer not to talk about it, so quit trying to make me.

5:01 PM, EST

Maybe I overreacted. After all, you guys are only trying to help. So if you insist, I'll tell you what happened.

I'M A WASHUP AT AGE 12 and $^{351}/_{365}$ths, that's what happened!!!

PS—That reminds me, only 14 shopping days left until my birthday.

5:18 PM, EST

Forgive me for that little outburst. I'm just so used to being loved and admired that this whole—how shall I put it—"being a loser" thing is all very new to me. I'll start slow:

It was the worst of times.

It was the worst of times.

It was the age of yuckiness.

It was the age of blech.

It was the first day of school.

Everyone in my homeroom class seemed thrilled to see each other. There was lots of hugging and kissing and shrieking with joy. They all exchanged expensive gifts from faraway places like Bali and Ibiza and the Epcot Center.

In the front center of the room stood four girls. They seemed to be the popular girls. Something about the way they looked so pretty and happy and well dressed. And the way the rest of the kids were content just watching them be pretty and happy and well dressed.

The prettiest and happiest and most well dressed of all is named Fiona. I think she's the main girl. She brought each of her friends their very own red leather bowling-bag purse, monogrammed in pink. You guys would have loved them. And it seemed like everything she said made her friends break out into fits of laughter. Either they were kissing up to her because of the bags or she's got a bright future as a stand-up comedienne.

But me? I stood alone in the corner, wishing I were one of them and trying to figure out what face to make. Then, just as I had landed on the perfect one (plain, but with the corners of my mouth slightly upturned to indicate that I was *glad* to be standing alone in the corner), I heard someone calling out my name. Really loudly.

At first I was excited. Someone wanted to talk to me! Turns out, my excitement was for nothing. It was only Jeremy Craine, that guy I told you about from my mother's wedding. His dad is Horse Ass's, I mean Horace's, business partner. He's the one who asked me to slow dance with him, and then in the middle of our dance, he did this trick where he turned his upper eyelids inside out. He thought it looked really funny. But really, it looked like he needed to be rushed to the hospital.

"Hey, Rae," he said. I could tell he was really proud of the rhyme. "Look what I got for you."

It was a can of chocolate-covered macadamia nuts. What could be more humiliating? Here everyone else was exchanging exotic gifts and red leather bags, and this joker gives me a can of chocolate-covered macadamia nuts? I know people like to pretend those nuts are from Hawaii and pass them off as souvenirs, but they're really from Pathmark and everyone knows it. Plus I'm allergic to them.

"Thanks, Jeremy, these are really great," I said. Then I shoved them in my bag so no one would see.

"Aren't you going to open them?" he asked, shouting at the top of his lungs. So he bought me a can of nuts—did the entire seventh grade need to know about it?

I opened the can as quickly as I could and poured some into his palm. Then I covered the can with the plastic lid and put it back in my bag.

"Don't you want some?" he asked, his voice even louder this time.

I didn't want to hurt the guy's feelings, but he gave me no choice.

"Not to be rude, but I'm allergic. Do you want them back?"

"That's okay; give them to your mom or something," he answered, looking kind of hurt. Which doesn't make any sense. People don't choose their allergies.

"I will. Thanks, Jeremy," I said, feeling kind of bad. Then the bell rang, which was a lucky thing. "See you later. . . ."

I suppose I *could* have taken a bite out of one of the nuts, but what if I had gotten sick? Wouldn't he have felt worse? Plus the longer I stood talking to him, the louder he would have gotten until there was no one left who hadn't noticed us together.

As it is, I'm sure most of them already did. Now what if everyone thinks I'm his girlfriend? If I'm going out with Jeremy, then no other guy will ask me out.

Plus he's nice and all, but what if he's a dork? It's so hard to tell here. In Berkeley you could see just by the way someone dressed. If a boy's shirt was tucked in, that was a telltale sign. But here there's a dress code. No sneakers. Collared shirts and sweaters for girls. Sweaters or shirts and ties for boys. So when it's warm out, they all look like dorks. I could go a whole semester without knowing.

Either way, it's only my first day at a new school—way too early to send out a message to everyone that I'm already taken. Especially by someone who thinks allergy-inducing snacks from the supermarket are exotic.

After Jeremy gave me the gift, I figured I'd lay low during lunch. In case he wanted me to sit next to him. So, I sat in the stairwell behind the auditorium and ate the chocolate off my macadamias all by my lonesome.

Let's review my first day of school:

1. I did not get expensive gifts.

2. No one talked to me.

3. Except Jeremy.

4. Now everyone thinks I'm his wife, which means no boy will ever ask me out.

5. I risked my health by eating chocolate contaminated with macadamia poisoning.

This is *so* not the way it was meant to be. With my metallic underwear and vitamin-A-smooth complexion, I was supposed to take Franklin Academy by storm. How did it go so wrong? And more importantly, how do I get my hands on one of those red bags?

Comments:

Logged in at 7:17 PM, EST

<u>kweenclaudia</u>: let's get one thing straight. you, raisin rodriguez, are not allergic to macadamia nuts. the reason you got sick that time I brought them back from my trip to hawaii (and i did not get them at the pathmark. i got them at the airport) is because you ate the entire jar in one sitting.

Logged in at 7:25 PM, EST

<u>PiaBallerina</u>: Don't worry, Raisy Mae. First days are always rough. What does Jeremy look like anyway? Is he cute?

Wednesday, September 15

7:06 AM, EST

Kitty Kats,

P, in answer to your question regarding whether Jeremy's cute or not: Jeremy is a freckle face. This is not opinion. This is fact. Not that there's anything wrong with it, but I've never been able to look at all those dots for very long without getting dizzy. So basically, I'll have to take some Dramamine, have a look, and get back to you.

I wish you guys were here. Then we could all take Dramamine and look at Jeremy's face together.

12:03 PM, EST

I just discovered the school's computer room. I can come here during lunch and write you guys. Which is a good thing since eating lunch takes only four minutes, leaving a friendless person such as myself with forty-one minutes to stare at the cafeteria wall. . . . Philadelphia might be the City of Brotherly Love, but it's also the City of Raisinly Indifference.

Not that I really have a right to complain when there are so many who've had it worse.

Take Gordo, for instance. The first monkey in space. You remember, we learned about him in history last year. The Defense Department sent him on a space ship around the earth. All by himself. No friends, no monogrammed bags, no one to make out with. That's seriously lonely. Okay, they probably didn't feed him chocolate-covered macadamia nuts, and he probably never ever had to worry about what face to make, but it had to have been awful. And that didn't stop him. He never let his fear bring him down. He just met his destiny and soldiered on.

From now on I'm going to try and be more like Gordo. So what if I take my meals alone and suffer from deadly allergies? If Gordo could brave his way through outer space, I can brave my way through Franklin Academy.

4:11 PM, EST

Life may not be an endless series of freckles and airport-purchased snacks after all. Today in earth science, I discovered that I have a lot in common with Fiona Small (the girl who brought the red leather bags for all her friends) and her best friend, Hailey Sherman. I guess you could say we have a similar way of looking at things. I've always known we were meant to be friends. Always since yesterday, that is.

There I was, listening to our teacher, Mr. Ferguson, droning on about sediment production and rock erosion. I was so bored, I wanted to unscrew my head and throw it at him. But just in the nick of time, Fiona handed me a note to pass to Hailey. It was like she was an angel, sent down to earth to protect me from myself.

Naturally, I took a peek at the note before passing it over. It said, *Why does Mr. Ferguson have pubic hair coming out of his ears?* An excellent question. One I had mulled over myself. I knew that girl had a good head on her shoulders.

Before passing the note to Hailey, I thought I should offer my own thoughts concerning the Ferguson hair matter. Show her how like-minded we all are. So I added in, *Wonder if he hears with his you-know-what,* before passing the note along.

Pretty sharp, huh?

I thought so too.

Unfortunately my little quip never made it to Hailey. Ferguson caught me mid-pass and confiscated the note.

"Raisin, if I catch you passing notes again, I'm going to give the whole class a pop quiz," he started. "Is that what you want?"

Of course that wasn't what I wanted. I wanted him to give the note back to Hailey so she could see how funny I am and tell Fiona.

"No, sir," I said, praying he wouldn't open the note.

He didn't. Chucked it right into the garbage. Can you believe it? If it were me, I'd have read the note right away. I guess when you have weirdly placed body hair, you learn to protect yourself from the painful truth.

By this time I'm sure half the class hated me for putting them at risk for a pop quiz. But I was helping Fiona out and that's what I cared about most. Friends need to stick together. Even if one of the friends doesn't know the other exists yet.

I spent the rest of the class imagining what I'd say after Fiona thanked me. "Oh, it was nothing." Or, "I'd risk anything just to have you utter my name." Or, "Buy me one of those red leather bags and we'll call it even."

But the moment never came. She never said a word to me. I even walked alongside her, just to jog her memory. Gave her a little wave. But she never looked my way.

I wondered if maybe she felt bad for getting me into trouble. I had to tell her that it was okay. But as I opened my mouth to call out her name, I overheard her say something that gave me second thoughts. Really frightened me. Sent chills up my spine, frankly.

She put her hands over her eyes, and . . .

Oh no. Wait. Not again!

Please excuse the interruption. Countess, my stepsister's irritating pet, is scratching at my door. Pet *what* is what I'd like to know. Samantha claims she's a poodle, but I'm not buying it. First of all, she's way too tall. Almost as tall as I am. And she has magenta manicured nails and wears bows over her ears and on top of her head. No self-respecting dog would stand for that kind of abuse. My guess is that she's either a polar bear with a bad perm or a short person in a dog suit paid by Samantha to annoy me so I'll move back to Berkeley.

Anyway, I think Countess has a drinking problem. She always needs to be walked. And since half the time no one's home but me, it's always me who's walking her.

Please hold . . .

Comments:

Logged in at 7:12 PM, EST

<u>PiaBallerina</u>: Raisin. Come back. You left us hanging. . . . What did Fiona say that sent chills up your spine?

8:12 PM, EST

So sorry, Kitties! I meant to get right back to my story. But I got detained. . . .

On my way out to walk Countess, my mother called to say she was going to be a little late for dinner (again!) and to ask me how my day went.

"Fine," I said. It was a little white lie, but I didn't see the point in interrupting her important businesswoman life by telling her the truth—that deep down I was suffering a pain so sharp it cut me where I live. Yes, even though she ruined my life, I saw no need to burden her with my agony.

But then I accidentally burst into hysterical tears and she saw through my little charade.

"Oh, honey. I guess you had a hard day. I'm so sorry that I'm working late again tonight. Is there anything I can do to make you feel better?" she asked.

"I don't think so," I said.

"Anything at all?"

"Well"—I hesitated—"there is one thing. . . ."

"What?"

"Maybe you could buy me some new clothes?"

She paused for a few seconds. I thought I had blown it by asking for too much. But then she said, "I suppose that's reasonable. Since I won't be home on time, why don't you stop at Giselle's and buy yourself a nice out-fit? Use the emergency credit card I gave you. And don't forget to show the salesperson my permission note."

"I won't," I said.

"And maybe tomorrow night, you and I can take a look at the list of after-school activities. See if there's anything that might interest you. When I was in seventh grade, I really got into—"

"Okay, Mom, sounds good. Talk to ya later."

I didn't mean to cut her off. But really, who needs after-school activities when you're wearing a fabulous new outfit?

Make that outfits.

Okay, so maybe I went a little overboard in my purchases, but as it turns out, I really need them. What I was starting to tell you before is that after earth science, I overheard Fiona saying something that really spooked me.

I noticed that she was covering her eyes with her hands and Hailey asked her what was wrong.

"I'm sorry," Fiona said. "It's that weirdo Kim Weingarten's skirt. It's so last century, it makes my eyes hurt."

"Well, maybe one person's 'so last century' is another's 'last-century chic,'" Hailey said, giggling.

The offending skirt was black gauze and went almost to that girl Kim's ankles. The skirt I had on was very similar, only I prefer the term "last-century chic." The point is, it frightens me to think of what could have happened if I had spoken to Fiona in that condition.

Like I said, chilling . . .

At least now that I'm learning how to dress for success in Philadelphia, the threat of danger has passed. Still, if I want to make friends with Fiona and Hailey, it seems wise to start with Hailey first. Then work my way up to Fiona later. Maybe Fiona was just having a bad day, but for now, Hailey seems . . . less picky.

It's almost like Hailey's the Philadelphia version of you, Pi, and Fiona's the Philadelphia version of you, Claud!

PS—I dumped Book Cover boy. It just wasn't working. He never wanted to go out and do things.

Don't worry, I let him down easy.

Comments:
Logged in at 10:13 PM, EST

<u>PiaBallerina</u>: Rae-rae, are you sure your mom won't be mad at you?

PS—What does Hailey look like?

Logged in at 10:18 PM, EST

<u>kweenclaudia</u>: sometimes you gotta live life on the edge p . . . sooo
rae . . . what'd ya get? what'd ya get?

Thursday, September 16

7:06 AM, EST

Kitties and Gentlemen,

Allow me to present:

The Raisin Rodriguez Fall Line
(*A Work in Progress*)

Look #1
Sassy student:
Plaid miniskirt

Angora short-sleeve crewneck sweater
Black knee-hi boots

Look #2
From classroom to dinner:
Gray satin cargo pants
Gray wool sleeveless turtleneck
Black high-heeled work boots

Look #3
For lazy, come-what-may days:
Chocolate-brown velour hoodie
Matching sweatpants with the word *bum* embroidered on the bum
Turquoise tank
Brown-and-turquoise Pumas

Look #4
For those I-just-want-to-blend-in-like-a-sheep days:
V-necked black sweater (with a detachable pink fabric flower to be attached once I figure out why it's suddenly fashionable to dress like Grandma Betty)
Low-slung jeans (consult your local plumber's butt crack for correct placement)
Old-skool Adidas

And my personal favorite:

Look #5
Evening elegance:
Fuschia sequined shell
Matching net ballet-skirt, tea length
Matching satin mules with kitten (kitten!) heels
False eyelashes

Today Raisin will sport look #1, sassy student. It says, "I'm playful, yet not to be toyed with." It says, "I have style, but I don't need to work at it." It says, "I used to dress like that weirdo Kim Weingarten, but now I've seen the light." It says, "Hailey! Please notice me."

Once Hailey sees me in my outfit, she'll want to know where I got it, and before long we'll be finishing each other's sentences.

Off to meet my public.

PS—Almost forgot, P—Hailey's really pretty. She has straight long brown hair with bangs, big brown eyes. And she's tall, thin, and very clean. Yesterday I saw her eating a bag of Cheez Doodles and she didn't get any crumbs on her clothes or even a speck of orange around her mouth.

. . . Don't know how she does it.

7:07 PM, EST

WHY? WHY? WHY?

7:08 PM, EST

FOR THE LOVE OF GOD, WHY?

7:09 PM, EST

WHY.
DOES.
THAT.
WOMAN.
CONTINUE
TO.
TRY.
AND.
RUIN.
ME?

IS IT NOT ENOUGH THAT SHE DRAGGED ME ALL THE WAY ACROSS THE COUNTRY TO LIVE IN THIS ONE-CREAM-CHEESE TOWN?

OR THAT SHE DIVORCED MY ONE AND ONLY FAVORITE FATHER, MARRIED A STRANGE LITTLE MAN (WHICH MEANS THAT SHE WILL NEVER GET BACK TOGETHER WITH MY FATHER), FORCED ME TO MOVE INTO SAID STRANGE MAN'S HOUSE WITH HIS PRISSY DAUGHTER AND HER EVEN MORE PRISSY DOG?

OR THAT SHE TOOK ME AWAY FROM MY BEST FRIENDS IN THE WHOLE WIDE WORLD?

THE ANSWER IS NO. IT'S NOT ENOUGH. BECAUSE (okay, no more caps, all this yelling is wearing me out) now that I've figured out that if I dress more like the other girls, I'll fit in better, she's taking away my fashion freedom.

The second she laid eyes on me walking into the kitchen—instead of breathing in the beauty that is sassy student and the way it brings out the brown in my hair, the brown in my eyes, and yes, the brown in my skin tone—she had a full-on maximum-strength conniption.

"Raisin Ramona Rodriguez, what in heaven's name are you wearing?"

"The outfit you told me to buy at Giselle's," I answered.

"I most certainly did not tell you to buy *that* outfit," she said, pointing a very pointy finger at me. "That skirt is way too short and those boots are way too high. You look like a . . . Just take it off! Immediately!"

"But I like it!" I said, pleading.

"Raisin, you march right up those stairs and change out of those clothes this instant. I will not have my daughter walking around half naked, looking like she's asking for trouble!" she shouted.

She wasn't even making sense. I wasn't asking for trouble. I was asking for love.

Then, as if my mother weren't angry enough, Lola came downstairs wearing the pink sequined shell. Although on her it was more like a dress. She just waddled into the room like a Teletubby with good taste, and when my mother asked her where she got the top, she sang like a canary.

"Raisin, is your sister telling the truth? Did you buy more than one outfit? Because I only recall giving you permission to buy one outfit!"

"But you haven't even seen the other outfits. Shouldn't you give them a chance?"

That last comment almost put her over the edge. It made her nostrils flare up to the size of Oreos. I was so afraid she'd start throwing things, I picked up a box of Fruity Pebbles and used it as a shield.

Nothing was thrown, but she did order me to change my clothes and put them back neatly in their bags so that she could return them. Then she informed me that I'd be eating dinner at Jeremy's because she and Horace have a late meeting. That's the third time she's missing dinner this week!

"And as punishment, you'll have to walk Countess for two weeks."

Punishment? Was she kidding me? If walking Countess is a punishment, then I've been on punishment since the day we got here. And besides,

wasn't sending me to Jeremy's punishment enough?
Jeez . . .

All I know is that my dad never would have forced
me to return the clothes. He would have gotten how
important they are. He's a really understanding person.
Maybe he learned it from teaching yoga. All that deep
breathing, and stretching, and saying things like,
"Wherever you go, there you are. . . ."

Sometimes I really wish my parents would have
decided to let me live with him. But they were both so
positive I'd be happier living with my mom. I guess
that's understandable. . . . Don't I seem happier?

. . .Time to say goodbye to the Raisin Rodriguez fall
line. I'm thinking I'll wear my denim mini with a pink
polo. . . . Not as fabulous as sassy student, but not as
friend retardant as the gauze skirt.

PS I'm keeping the removable fabric flower. Just in
case I ever do figure out why it's fashionable. Oh, and
the false eyelashes. Can't give those back—Lola stuck
one up her nose.

9:20 PM, EST

Freckles aside, what I learned about Jeremy tonight
is that he can be kind of fun.

And kind of *not*.

For example, on the walk home from school, we passed one of his neighbors, mowing the lawn.

"Why is that guy wearing a pink skirt?" I asked, noticing how short the grass is kept here.

"That's not a guy," Jeremy said. "That's Mrs. Hunt."

"Are you sure?" I asked. Because Mrs. Hunt looks like a mister to me."

"I know. But she's definitely a she."

"That's so weird," I said.

"I know," he agreed. Then he got quiet for about a minute as we waited for a light to turn green.

"I've always wanted to prank call her and just keep referring to her as Mr. Hunt. Even after she corrected me. Pretend I was taking a survey on aftershave or favorite football teams or something like that. . . ."

What a brilliant idea, I thought. Jeremy had never made more sense in his life. Suddenly I was seeing him with new eyes.

"Let's do it!" I said.

"We can't actually *do* it, " he said. "It's too mean."

"Okay," I said, "then we'll do it to someone random. It's funny no matter who we call."

He agreed.

So when we got to his house, we took out the phone book, found someone named Mrs. Mann, and dialed her number. We thought it would be extra funny because if she said, "But I'm a woman," we could keep saying, "But your name is Mann."

Get it? *Mann.*

Jeremy dialed, but when Mrs. Mann answered the phone, he hung up. *Okay, fine,* I thought. *He's a little nervous, we'll try once more.*

We chose another name, he dialed, and when the person answered, Jeremy hung up the phone again. *Okay,* I thought, *maybe I should do it.*

So this time I dialed, but when the person picked up, Jeremy pulled out the phone cord.

"It's just too nasty. Why don't we call someone and pretend we're real estate agents trying to sell them a house?" he asked.

"Okay, I'm with ya so far . . . and then what?"

"And then," he started, "then . . . we . . . hang up."

"What's funny about that?" I asked.

"I dunno," he answered.

I'm sure you can imagine my disappointment. I was all ready for a gigantic yet purely innocent laugh at some poor unsuspecting soul's expense, and Jeremy had to ruin it by being *nice.*

Thankfully, his mom called us to dinner just then. Tuna casserole—the good kind, made with tomato sauce instead of barfy mushroom soup. I liked her a lot. She was really friendly and she works as a buyer for

Neiman Marcus, so she wore the coolest outfit—a pink plaid jacket with a gold chain belt over jeans.

. . . Maybe she'd know where I could find one of those red bags.

After dinner Jeremy walked me home, and on the way his mother called to remind him about a dentist appointment. I noticed that his cell is one of those camera phones. So I had the idea to find people doing embarrassing things and take pictures of them without them noticing.

Thankfully, this time Mr. Nicey Nice was into it.

We passed a guy sitting on a bus stop bench picking his nose, so we took a picture of him. Then we passed a couple smooching in a parked car, so we shot that. And then right around the corner from my house, we saw this old lady walking her cat on a leash, so we took a picture of her too!

"Let's e-mail them to the *Chestnut Hill Troubadour*," he said. "We can do it right now, straight from the phone."

Brilliant! I thought. *It's one great idea after another with this guy.* So we sent the pictures off and made like we were big-time reporters or something. I was all ready to reconsider my feelings about Jeremy.

Except that when we got to my front door, he had to ruin it. Again.

"Hey, you think the *Troubadour* will publish our pictures?" he asked at the top of his lungs. I was already in enough trouble with my mom. The last thing I needed was for her to find out what Jeremy and I had been up to.

"Of course not. But could you lower your voice? I don't want my mom to find out."

"Okay, sorry," he said.

I think I might have embarrassed him. But seriously, he's got to do something about that loudyitis, soon.

What if he has a relapse tomorrow at school? What if he sees me in the cafeteria and yells out something like, "It was really fun making immature prank phone calls and then chickening out in the end," or worse, "Hey, Raisin, thanks for last night."

I think I'm going to skip lunch again just in case. I feel bad because he's so nice. But I'm worried about people getting the wrong idea.

Comments:

Logged in 11:03 PM, EST

<u>kweenclaudia</u>: instead of skipping lunch, you could get one of those "i'm with stupid" t-shirts and write in the word *not* between the words *i'm* and *with*. you could wear it whenever you're around ol' jeremy. just make sure you always sit with the arrow facing toward him. then everyone will know you're *not* with him.

Logged in at 11:30 PM, EST

PiaBallerina: Raisin, you shouldn't worry so much about what people think. Besides, I like Jeremy. He sounds really sweet.

Logged in at 11:45 PM, EST

kweenclaudia: if you follow p's advice, all you'll get is the satisfaction of knowing you're doing the right thing. but if you follow mine, you'll have the satisfaction of knowing you've solved a difficult dilemma through the magic of fashion.

Friday, September 17

7:03 AM, EST

My Fellow Felines,

No need for a catfight; you both gave excellent advice. I'll stop worrying *and* I'll get one of those T-shirts, just in case.

4:28 PM, EST

P, you'll be very proud of me. I ate lunch with Jeremy and I didn't even wear the T-shirt. (Mostly because I don't have it yet.)

It all started because Sparkles cut right in front of me on the lunch line. He has this way of appearing out of nowhere.

"Hey, New Girl," he said, tugging at my hair. "I hope you like tuna casserole."

"So *that's* what that is. Jeez, I just had some for dinner last night."

"I hope it was better than the one they serve here. They make it with mushroom soup."

"Barfy," I said.

"Yuh-huh," he said. "Get used to it. It's like the only recipe they have in their cookbook."

Just then Jeremy of all people got in line behind us, catching me off guard.

"Raisin, look! Tuna casserole, just like last night!" he said, sounding very excited.

Thankfully Sparkles didn't ask about last night. He must have grown bored with the all the TC talk because as soon as Jeremy brought it up, he left.

So there I was stuck with the loudyitis patient and nothing to eat.

"You vant an egg?" asked Esther the cafeteria lady. She's from Transylvania.

It just so happened, I did vant an egg. Jeremy went the cottage-cheese-and-peaches route.

I can't believe he hasn't figured out yet that cottage cheese is just milk nobody wanted. I was dying to tell him this, but sometimes you just have to let people learn from their own mistakes.

"Wanna sit with me?" he asked.

The question I'd been afraid of. I didn't know what

to tell him. I couldn't exactly say that I'd prefer to eat all alone in a cinder-block stairwell.

"I would," I said. "But I'm already sitting with. . ." I had no idea how to complete that sentence. I hardly know anyone's names yet.

Finally one came to me. It stuck in my brain because I had never heard anything quite like it before. "Galenka Boxofchocolates from my math class . . ."

"Galenka Popodakolis?" he corrected. "You know, her translator doesn't sit with her at lunch."

Turns out, Galenka wasn't the best choice. She's a foreign exchange student who only speaks Greek and . . . math.

"Translator? You mean she was speaking to me in Greek? Jeez, I must have completely misunderstood. I hope she wasn't trying to tell me she was in some kind of trouble or something. For all I know, she was asking me to perform the Heimlich maneuver or mouth-to-mouth. Well, in that case . . ." I said, and doing the only thing I could do at that moment, I followed him to his table.

A bunch of his friends were already seated there. They all kind of blended into one except for this guy Roger, who stuck out because of his height. He was extremely large for a twelve-year-old. Which makes me wonder if he's been a seventh grader once or twice before.

Lunch with Jeremy's friends was very educational. Here's what I learned: Boys can be really dopey.

You know how they spent their lunch period? Playing table hockey with a bottle cap, that's how. Or more accurately, playing table hockey with a bottle cap and sweating.

They kept asking me if I wanted to play and seemed genuinely perplexed that I didn't. Was it really so difficult to understand? Their collective sweat was forming a puddle at the bottom of the bottle cap!

If only I were already friends with Fiona and Hailey, I'd have been spending my lunch period productively. From what I could see, they appeared to be swapping mani/pedis with the two other girls they hang out with. Or, more accurately, Hailey and the two friends appeared to be giving one to Fiona. In raciest red of all colors! At one point Hailey took the polish and used it to paint a pair of lips on the platform heels of Fiona's sandals. What a great idea! I must go home and copy her immediately.

. . . It all brought me back to the days when you guys and I would polish each other's nails.

But I wasn't going to let it get to me. I was going to use this time wisely—to find out more about those four girls.

"You guys, I have a question," I said.

No one responded, so I asked again.

"Hey, you guys, can I ask you something?" I said it three more times, and still no one answered me. I guess I can't really blame them. They were deep in a very intellectual debate over who gets more hotties: quarterbacks or rock stars.

Finally I just blurted it out.

"You guys, what are the names of the two girls sitting with Hailey and Fiona?"

As soon as those boys heard the name Fiona, they stopped the game dead in its tracks. Some of them looked down at the floor or scratched their heads. Some stole a quick glance at Fiona as if to make sure she wasn't listening. They all began to sweat twice as hard.

"Fiona who?" Roger asked.

"Yeah, which Fiona do you mean?" asked a different sweaty boy.

I'm pretty sure there's only one Fiona in the grade. Why were they acting so freaky?

"You know exactly which Fiona she's talking about. She's talking about the Fiona that you LOVE," said a third sweaty boy to his sweaty friend.

"No, *you* do."

"No, *you* do."

As the rest of them broke out into a chorus of "No,

you do's," Jeremy sat quietly, kind of gazing in Fiona's direction. If anyone loves her, I'm putting my money on him.

So Fiona Small's the sex symbol of Franklin Academy. Makes perfect sense. She's beautiful and funny and has friends who'll give her mani/pedis without expecting her to return the favor.

Once Jeremy pulled it together, he told me the other two girls' names. The redhead is Bliss DiMarco and the one with short brown hair is Madison Ames.

Then he gave Fiona one more look of love.

Boy, has he got it bad.

8:04 PM, EST

I tried painting a pair of lips on my brown platforms—but it came out looking like a red pepper.

Comments:

Logged in at 8:58 PM, EST

<u>kweenclaudia</u>: rae, we never polished each other's nails . . . though when we were in kindergarten, you did take a sip from my mother's purple passion polish thinking it was grape juice.

Logged in at 9:07 PM, EST

<u>PiaBallerina</u>: But we did cut each other's hair that one time last year. And a fine job we did if I remember correctly . . .

Monday, September 20

7:03 AM, EST

Kittens,

Pi! You inspired me to cut my own bangs. Unfortunately, I think I really screwed up. Now they're way too short. I look like the girl in the movie who cuts her hair with a kitchen knife because she has a nervy after her boyfriend dumps her. Then she looks so crazy, they lock her up in the loony bin!

How can I hope to impress the Fiona and Haileys looking like this?

4:28 PM, EST

I'll tell you how. By being the brilliant genius that I am.

This morning during math class, I found myself distracted by the scent of cinnamon. It was very strong, yet very delicious. I took a look around me, and it seemed to be coming from the direction of the boy seated to my left. His name is CJ. He's kind of rumpled and sloppy and not the cinnamon type at all, though, so I wasn't sure.

I kept looking around a bit more, and that's when I happened to notice Hailey's algebra homework. Poor thing had $x = 215,268,4024$ as her answer. First of all, I'm pretty sure two hundred and fifteen million, two hundred and sixty-eight *thousand,* four *thousand* and twenty-four isn't a number. Second of all, the correct answer was 3.

I really felt for her. Especially since the teacher announced a quiz on Friday. It just doesn't seem right. Here she's got so many things going for her—her friendships, her kindness, her red leather bag (which looked so good against her black pencil-skirt). And then there's this pesky algebra issue throwing the whole picture out of balance.

No way can I allow my future friend to fail a math quiz. The only thing to do is to invite her over to my house for a study session.

Gotta go! I have to get started on my list of discussion topics for Hailey's visit. The last thing I'd want is to run out of things to talk about. Imagine bringing her all the way over here only to be plagued by sudden-onset boringitis!

Bye for now!

PS—I need my bangs to grow in by Tuesday. I've tried tugging at them but can only keep it up for brief stretches. If only I could find tiny weights and attach them to the ends of my hair . . .

7:15 PM, EST

Have been hanging upside down to induce bang

growth. Too busy for pronoun use as am in preparation for life of wild popularity.

Talking Points for Thursday
(To be used as backup material or in the case of conversation lag)

1. Frenching—Why less tongue is more (basic, but useful as an icebreaker)
2. Miniskirts over pants—Attractive look or fashion magazine conspiracy?
3. Mary-Kate or Ashley?

I like this list. It asks the questions on the minds of seventh graders today.

7:23 PM, EST

This is a terrible list! I'm a social zero! Hailey will never be my friend.

7:27 PM, EST

I took a deep breath and reread the list. It's still terrible. Maybe I should have my dad FedEx me that picture of him teaching yoga to Madonna. I could show it to Hailey and make her think I'm really important. A person to be seen with.

7:28 PM, EST

What a dork I am! Going to such great lengths to get someone to like me is sad. Oh, the embarrassment! Just thinking about it gives me that awful potato-salad feeling in the back of my throat. Hailey will either like me for who I am, or she won't. Take me or leave me.

8:30 PM, EST

What if she leaves me?

She can't. I'm Raisin Rodriguez, math genius, brilliant conversationalist, and close personal friend to Madonna.

Okay . . . wait . . . I'm losing my train of thought. Countess is pawing at my door and . . . wait . . . what was I talking about? . . . Oh yes . . . my greatness . . .

The point is that . . . OH MY GOD!

I haven't shared the big gossip yet. . . .

The other day I was walking Countess, and I noticed something unusual when she lifted her leg to pee. I noticed that she's a boy. You heard me. Countess Louise Bennett, canine pet to Samantha Louise Bennett, is one hundred percent male. I guess I never looked before because I don't like to pay her too much attention.

As you might guess, I found this very curious. So when my mom got home from work (in time for dinner for a change), I found her in the kitchen and asked her about it.

"Hey, Mom, I was just wondering. Is it my imagination or is Countess a boy?" I asked.

My mom looked pretty uncomfortable as she took the bag of groceries she'd been unloading and set it aside on the counter.

"Raisin," she said. "Take a seat."

I felt nervous as I sat down. Like my mom was about to tell me that Countess had a terrible disease or something.

"Raisin, this may sound strange to you, but it's not your imagination. Countess is a boy." She said it in a whisper. "After her parents' divorce," Mom continued, "Samantha really wanted a female dog. A female white standard poodle, to be specific. But when the stores were out of females, she settled on a male dog. Your stepdad had no idea she was planning on disguising the dog as a girl, but he didn't try to talk her out of it. Sam's a very sensitive girl and he didn't want to upset her any more than she already had been."

Before I could even comment, Mom added, "But don't say anything about it, okay? Your stepdad would like us all to just go along with it."

I just thought Samantha was weird because she's more into school than friends. But this dog business makes her ten times weirder. See what divorce does to kids? She'll be okay, though. She's got looks and intelligence . . . and that weird circle of brainiacs leaving all those messages for her on her cell phone.

Cripes! There goes Countess again. Can't he wait? I'm trying to immortalize him with my words. . . . Oh, jeez . . .

OH MY GOD, he's completely lost it. Someone should loosen that bow on his head. He just came barreling through my door so quickly, you'd think the pound was after him. Now he's standing in the corner, whining at me like a little girl. He's starting to believe the hype!

I guess I should walk him. He probably needs to pee or find his dignity or something.

8:33 PM, EST

Never mind. Countess didn't have to go out at all. He was just running away from Lola. She keeps calling him "horsie" and trying to ride him bareback. I think it's Lola who needs to be walked.

Comments:

Logged in at 9:10 PM, EST

<u>kweenclaudia</u>: so basically, countess is a doggy in drag! i love it!

ps—don't worry about your list. it'll work fine. just wondering if frenching is the best topic for you. wouldn't it be better to discuss something you know about?

Logged in at 9:12 PM, EST

<u>PiaBallerina</u>: **Don't listen to Claudia. She's just jealous because you're trying to make new friends.**

Tuesday, September 21

12:38 PM, EST

Good morning,

It's freezing at school today! During homeroom, they announced that they can't get the air conditioner to stop running. As a former Berkeley resident, I'm not a big fan of the cold. I don't think my boobs are either, based on the way my nips are behaving. They're practically bursting through my clothes. I think it's their way of saying, "Get us out of this city." It got so bad in math class, I had to hold off on talking to Hailey about coming over Thursday night. Wouldn't have wanted her to get the wrong idea . . .

Now I'm wearing my coat and a hat, scarf, and pair of mittens I borrowed from the lost and found. I hope it doesn't stay this cold. I can't keep walking around like a lost Inuit.

Make that a lost Inuit with mental patient bangs.

PS—I do so know about Frenching, Claudia.

Comments:

Logged in at 8:30 PM, EST

<u>kweenclaudia</u>: **frenching with your cousin doesn't count.**

Logged in at 8:31 PM, EST

<u>PiaBallerina</u>: It does if he's cute. And Raisin's cousin is way cute.

Logged in at 8:33 PM, EST

<u>kweenclaudia</u>: rae-rae, i think pia has something to tell you.

Logged in at 8:36 PM, EST

<u>PiaBallerina</u>: Claudia. You promised. . . . Oh, all right. I guess it was bound to come out sometime. Rae, I have a little crush on your cousin Danny . . . is that okay with you?

Wednesday, September 22

7:42 AM, EST

Pia! That's great. Although I did *not* french him, he's totally cute, especially when he plays basketball. And when he reads stories to his little brother. And when he sleeps. Not that I know what he looks like when he sleeps or anything. But you know . . . he just has that kind of face. Keep in mind, though, he tends to get potato chips stuck in his braces, so you might want to offer him a travel toothbrush.

And while you're at it, here's something else you might want to keep in mind:

(You too, Claud.)

Ladies, it's all about the bra. . . .

I put on a wool sweater and borrowed Samantha's

padded bra to protect against that unsightly nippyitis. And I must say, I'm really liking it. It's not white and cottony like the baby bras I've got but blue and silky like a mature person's bra. And it really does something for my shape. Makes me look almost like an adult-woman-type person—like I should be wearing slingbacks and carrying a purse . . . going to my job where I get to sit with my feet up on the desk and shout things like, "That's my final offer," into the phone before hanging up without saying goodbye.

Off to school. Wish Lola would stop wiping her peanut-butter-and-jelly hands all over my sweater. PB&J stains are not very adult.

4: 55 PM, EST

This bra has changed my life.

For one thing, it has a positive effect on the opposite sex. Today Mike Leary, an *eighth grader* who has math right before I do, spoke to me. He said, "Hey." I haven't had an older man interested in me since Thomas Dyson.

Before the padded bra, I couldn't get a seventh grader to breathe near me (well, except for Jeremy, who doesn't count) and now all of a sudden, I have eighth graders proposing, practically.

But more importantly, without the annoying nip trouble holding me back, I was able to approach Hailey Sherman.

Went right up to her after algebra and said, "Hailey, would you like to come over to my house to study for the algebra test?"

And without too long a pause (like eleven seconds) she said, "Maybe."

9:03 PM, EST

"Maybe" is good, right?

9:04 PM, EST

Unless, of course, it's bad.

9:23 PM, EST

Then again, who has time for *maybe?* I certainly don't. Not me. I'm wildly popular. Perhaps Hailey hasn't heard about me and Mike Leary?

11:31 PM, EST (aka can't fall asleep)

Could "maybe" be short for "maybe if you didn't have mental patient bangs"?

Comments:

Logged in at 11:45 PM, EST

<u>PiaBallerina</u>: I'm so glad you're okay about me and Danny. I really hope he likes me!

PS—Don't worry about Hailey. I'm sure she wants to come to

your house. She probably just has to check with her parents.

Logged in at 11:47 PM, EST

<u>kweenclaudia</u>: **that's nice of you to say, pi. but I think what rae really needs is a bra for her brain. To rein in the craziness.**

Thursday, September 23

2:33 AM, EST

So what if it means *no?* Her loss. We'll just see how far "maybe" and her ten-digit answer gets her.

BTW, good morning, Kitties, one and all. Hope you guys are enjoying a restful sleep. Someone should be.

PS—Of course Danny will like you, Pi.

7:15 AM, EST

I am dead meat. I am deader than dead.

Samantha's padded bra is gone!!! I've looked everywhere for it and it's nowhere to be found. And I swear I was trying so hard to be careful. I even slept in it last night. The only time it left my sight is when I showered, and maybe I should have gone without, but I didn't want to risk the possibility of stinkyitis on today of all days.

I don't know who could have taken it. It wasn't Samantha because she slept at a friend's house last night. It wasn't my mother because she's already left for work. It wasn't Lola because she's watching *Rugrats* and when that show's on, the house could burn down around her and she wouldn't budge. And it wasn't my stepdad because he's weird, but he's not that weird.

Samantha's gonna WHACK me when she finds out.

Fo' real, yo. (If I'm going to get into a girl fight, I have to start talking the talk.)

PS—Now might be a good time for me to mention that when I said I borrowed Samantha's bra, what I meant was "took without asking."

12:46 PM, EST

Maybe means *yes! Maybe* means *yes!*

And I didn't even have to ask. Hailey came up to me right before math class and said, "Okay, I'll come," and that was that. When you play it cool, *they* come to you.

Life is good.

(Not that good, though. Still haven't found the bra. I could be dead by sundown.)

7:28 PM, EST

If only *maybe* had meant *no* . . .

Then I wouldn't have blown my one chance at wild popularity. I'm a social washup less than two weeks into my Franklin Academy career. And it's all my mother's fault . . .

Everything started out fine enough. After dismissal, Hailey and I met in front of the school steps. I was cool, calm, and collected. I had my talking points handy just in case. (Turns out I didn't need them—Hailey's quite the Chatty Cathy. Not that I minded. I'm all about filling the silences.)

Most importantly, she didn't mention my bangs.

We got to my house. I took her into the kitchen and put out a very mature snack of Diet Coke and carrot sticks even though I'd been dreaming about Lola's Dunkaroos since breakfast. I got nervous when Countess started begging from Hailey, but it didn't bother her at all.

"I LOVE dogs, don't you?" she said.

"Of course . . . Who doesn't?" I answered.

Then I brought her up to my room so we could study. Countess followed us. Teaching Hailey algebra was going to require intense concentration, so when we got to my room, I shut the door. Countess was quiet for about seven minutes, and then just as we were settling in, he started doing the pawing thing again. I let it go on as long as I could, but after a while, the scratching got too loud. He needed a walk. And since I'm still on punishment, I couldn't ask Samantha to do it.

I apologized for the interruption and told Hailey she could wait for me in my room. Go through my CD collection

and listen to anything she wanted. But she said she preferred to come along. It was raining outside, so either she
really, really loves dogs, or she was avoiding Lola.

We grabbed our umbrellas and went outside. Then
we walked for a couple of blocks, but Countess
wouldn't . . . do his business. Apparently it wasn't a
tree or fire hydrant he was looking for—it was a nice
slab of cement.

See, Countess has a little problem with itchiness. In
a very personal and private area. And since he can't
use his paws to scratch there, he resorts to spinning
around and around on the area in question.

We kept walking. Countess kept spinning. Every
once in a while he'd get on all fours and run to catch
up with us. At some point he even got ahead of us.
That's when I noticed a little blue piece of I-don't-
know-what sticking out from his . . . ahem . . . area. At
first, I didn't think much of it. But then I realized it was
exactly the same color as Samantha's bra.

Could it be? Had Countess eaten Samantha's bra for
breakfast? Why would he do such a thing? And more
importantly, why was that overgrown fur ball trying to
mess me up ? A thorough investigation was in order,
but it couldn't be done in front of a dog lover like
Hailey.

There was only one thing to do.

I had to get rid of her.

"Hailey?" I said, but in the form of a question so as to sound super-duper polite. "I know this sounds crazy," I began, adding boo-boo eyes for effect, "but Countess is a very shy dog and feels unladylike pooping in front of guests. Would it be okay if we just met you back at my house?"

"Sure," Hailey said. She was probably relieved to be getting away from the spectacle.

As soon as the coast was clear, I put down my umbrella and leaned in to grab the evidence. But by that time, Countess was sitting and wouldn't get up. No matter how much I begged and pleaded. I even tried pulling him up by his front paws, but it was no use. Maybe he was punishing me for denying his femininity.

Minutes passed. I was getting drenched. Finally Countess gave in and stood up. I inspected the blue material. There was no question it belonged to the bra.

My first instinct was to ignore the situation in the hope it would go away. But my conscience wouldn't let me. What if Countess died of lingerie poisoning? The only choice was to remove the bra.

I took a deep breath and closed my eyes, pulling lightly at the fabric. At first nothing happened. But I kept at it, slowly but surely, one hand over the other, like a Girl Scout. . . . Shed a whole new light on the meaning of "be prepared."

I was *this* close to getting the whole thing out when I heard the sound of footsteps coming toward me. I prayed they didn't belong to Hailey. Or Samantha. Or anyone with eyes.

"What's taking so long?"

It was Hailey. I stalled for time. "Why'd you come back?" I asked.

"Because I saw your mom pulling into the driveway and I felt funny walking into your house without you."

As I racked my brain for a way to get rid of her again, something gave. The bra came loose and went flying out of Countess at like a hundred miles an hour. The impact threw me off balance and I went sliding on the slick cement, landing flat on my back.

I quickly threw the bra into the nearby front hedge, hoping Hailey wouldn't notice. But it was too late. Hailey saw the entire thing. Her face started turning shades of gray.

"I think I'm gonna throw up," Hailey said. This was not good. If she hated throwing up as much as I hated throwing up, she'd never forgive me.

"Try thinking nice thoughts," I offered. But it was no use.

"I just want to go home," she said. I couldn't really blame her.

Hailey had to stop off at my house to pick up her bag. As we walked over, the air was thick with silence. I broke it by asking her if she was worried about failing the algebra test.

"No," she said.

But she had to be. She was headed for flunkdom. And even though she was about to lose her lunch, I had to tell her this, as a friend.

"Hailey, I know we hardly know each other, but I think you should probably review inverse operations before tomorrow's test."

"Why? They're not that hard."

"Hailey, you don't have to be ashamed in front of me. I saw your math homework on Monday, and your answer was off by like two hundred million."

"Are you talking about that number that began with 215?" she asked.

"Yeah," I said, noting that for someone with poor math skills, she had an unusually good memory for numbers.

"That's Mike Leary's phone number. You *are* aware that 215 is the area code here in Philadelphia . . . ?"

I was. Until my need for Hailey's friendship turned my brain turned into thin air and seeped right through my ears.

I was so embarrassed, I didn't have time to dwell on the fact that Mike Leary was two-timing me.

"Then why'd you agree to come over and study?" I asked, foolishly hoping she'd say something about wanting to be my friend.

"Well . . . no offense, but I needed an excuse to get out of babysitting for my brother . . . ya know?"

Actually, Hailey, I don't.

If anyone from here invited me to her house, I'd be totally excited. (Other than Jeremy, who doesn't count as a school friend.)

Okay, maybe not that girl Kim Weingarten, who kind of frightens me even though we happen to have the same taste in skirts. She just sits in back of English class with her arms folded, wearing black lipstick and picking at her old mosquito bites until they bleed. Plus her friends are really weird. But anyone else. I swear.

I'm so tired of being the new girl. I'm tired of trying to make new friends. I mean, I like the Fiona and Haileys, but I'm always worried about what they're thinking. I never had to worry about what you guys thought. . . .

I wish lying in bed and eating bags of Sour Patch Kids were a job because then I could drop out of school and get an early start on my career.

How does one go on? What's the next step? And what will it take to get my mother to stop ruining my social life?

1. Again, let's review: She made me move here.

2. She made me take the clothes back to Giselle's. The very clothes that might have instantly won me Fiona and Hailey's affections.

3. In addition to making me take the clothes back, she gave me the punishment of having to walk Countess for two weeks.

4. And now Hailey thinks I'm repulsive.

Why doesn't my mom want me to have friends?

I think I'm going to be unfriendly to her until she improves her attitude.

8:02 PM, EST

Not too unfriendly, though—my birthday's coming up.

8:07 PM, EST

Which reminds me, only 5 more shopping days left until the big day.

Comments:
Logged in at 8:35 PM, EST

<u>PiaBallerina</u>: I know it seems awful now, but Hailey will forget about it all eventually. You know, just like I forgot about the cottage-cheese-and-bananas incident. I mean . . . you know what I mean.

Logged in at 8:37 PM, EST

<u>PiaBallerina</u>: I mean that . . . I heart you.

Logged in at 8:41 PM, EST

<u>kweenclaudia</u>: pia's right, rae. hailey'll forget eventually. in the meantime, all i can say is that my heart goes out to you. that must have been really poomiliating.

Logged in at 8:43 PM, EST

<u>PiaBallerina</u>: I think that's Claudia's way of saying she hearts you too.

PS—Rae! I can't believe I almost forgot! I've got some great gossip to cheer you up. Guess who got her period? Belinda Mulvaney! I think she's the first of all of our friends. Or at least the first to admit it!

Friday, September 24

7:07 AM, EST

Kitties,

Big Boobs Belinda got her period! I guess we should have seen that one coming.

I feel bad for her, though. I mean, once you get your period, it's pretty much downhill from there, right? The fun's over. All you've got to look forward to is high school, college, jobs, responsibility, and PMS every month.

Please tell BB my thoughts are with her.

12:23 PM, EST

I could barely look at Hailey during earth science today. And I know she must have told Fiona what happened. I'm not sure what tipped me off. It was either

A. The way they both giggled after I said hi to them on the way to my seat

or

B. The way they whispered to each other when I passed them on the way out of class.

5:46 PM, EST

I found the saddest picture of Gordo online. When they sent him into space, they dressed him in a tiny helmet and strapped him to a molded rubber bed with his knees drawn up to resist gravity. How could they have been so insensitive? That seems more like something Lola would do to one of her Ken dolls (never to Barbie, though) than something grown-ups would do to a helpless, innocent monkey.

It's good that I have all this time on my hands now. Otherwise I couldn't devote the proper time to honoring Gordo's memory. Picking up the slack for others who are too busy to think about martyred monkeys and other animals whose lives ended mercilessly and prematurely.

Saturday, September 25

5:05 PM, EST

Did I mention that Gordo was only one foot tall?

Sunday, September 26

6:27 PM, EST

Or that he was a squirrel monkey? Which is my second-favorite kind, next to Chunky Monkey . . .

Monday, September 27

4:48 PM, EST

Or that you can see how frightened he was just by looking at his picture?

Comments:

Logged in at 8:07 PM, EST

<u>PiaBallerina</u>: Raisin, I'm really sorry about Gordo, I truly am. But he's all you've talked about for four days. I know what happened to him is really sad, but he died almost fifty years ago, and there's really nothing you can do about it now. Besides, tomorrow is your birthday!

Logged in at 8:19 PM, EST

<u>kweenclaudia</u>: pia's right, raymundo. . . . wow—i have no desire to tease you about any of this . . . kind of a first for me. . . .

Tuesday, September 28

7:06 AM, EST

Happy birthday, dear me, happy birthday, dear me, happy birthday, dear me-ee, happy birthday, dear me.

So, I'm thirteen today. . . . Where does the time go?

You'll be happy to know, I've decided to put my grieving aside for the day and embrace the here and now. I'm sure Gordo would understand. Actually, I decided this last night at 9:54 PM, when I realized that I'd better call Jeremy if I didn't want to spend the day alone.

"Jeremy," I said, "tomorrow's my birthday."

"Oh, great, I'll bring a cake and we can celebrate with the guys at lunch," he said.

"Why not just make it a cupcake? And can we do it in the stairwell behind the gym? I don't really know those guys so well, so I'd rather it was just the two of us." I still don't want to give those guys reason to think I'm Jeremy's girlfriend.

"Sure, Raisin, whatever you want," he said.

"Great, Jeremy. Vanilla butter cream's my favorite." Just before I hung up, I added, "And no presents!"

Wouldn't have wanted a repetition of the macadamia nuts incident.

12:43 PM, EST

My birthday's going okay so far.

Got a ninety-two on my algebra quiz. Hailey got a ninety-six.

The teacher announced the names of everyone who got over a ninety. Besides me and Hailey, there were a few math geeks, Galenka Popodakolis, and that boy CJ, who is definitely the source of the cinnamon smell. When he walked by me to pick up his paper, I got a really strong whiff of it. I never met a boy who smelled like cinnamon before. It's kind of cute.

I noticed something new about him today. He's got the bluest eyes I've ever seen and eyelashes a mile long. I think he might be gorgeous.

I guess I never saw it before because he's always got his face buried in some picture he's drawing. Some kind of superhero, I think. Not Superman or Spider-Man or anyone famous. But one he made up, with scales and talons and a propeller on his head.

I've never seen anyone concentrate so hard. He's been working on the same picture since the first time I noticed him. Always adding in some extra detail, even though it's been looking finished for a while now. And he puts so much pressure on the pencil, I worry the point will break and ricochet off the page and into his eye.

He must be very shy. I've never even heard him speak. I think he works on his picture as an excuse not to look up. Which makes no sense. He should be show-ing off that face whenever possible.

I must get to the bottom of the CJ mystery. At least it'll give me something to do during math instead of wishing Hailey didn't hate me.

PS Jeremy surprised me with a vanilla cupcake at lunch! Never mind that he carried it to school on its side so that half the frosting ended up sticking to the inside of the box; it's the thought that counts.

Comments:

Logged in at 7:12 PM, EST
<u>kweenclaudia</u>: happy birthday raisin. and since it is your special day, i won't bother mentioning that once you tell someone to do some-thing, it doesn't count as a surprise anymore.

Logged in at 7:15 PM, EST
<u>PiaBallerina</u>: Hmmm . . . I wonder why CJ's so shy. . . . How was the rest of your day? Did you get our presents?

Wednesday, September 29

7:06 AM, EST
Kitty Cats,

Yes, Pia, I got your presents. Thank you sooooo much. I loved the Chia Pet and the can of sardines, and

I know the whoopee cushion will come in handy, but I think it's the tube of Preparation H that means the most to me. How'd ya know?

But the rest of my day was pretty lousy.

My mom took me out to Antonio's to celebrate my birthday. Italian—my favorite. Unfortunately she also brought along Horse Ass, Samantha, and Lola.

The waiter took our orders. Mom told me Lola had something special for me. Something glam, I hoped . . . or at least splashy.

But when Lola unzipped her lunch box to get at the "something special," my expectations were instantly lowered. Whatever it was, I knew it would smell like apple juice and cream cheese. It turned out to be a white paper hat from Krispy Kreme with the words *Happy Birthday Raisin* scribbled in brown crayon. The *B* in *Birthday* was backward, and she spelled *Raisin* with an *m* at the end.

"Thanks," I said, shoving the hat in my backpack. But that wasn't good enough for my mother. I could tell by the look she gave me. It was the same one she used when I tried to wear the sassy student outfit to school.

"Raisin, your sister made a big effort; the least you could do is show some gratitude and wear her birthday crown."

Big effort? How much effort did it take to scribble my name in crayon on a hat she got for free?

"I *am* grateful. I'm putting it in my scrapbook, right next to the paper plate she gave me for my birthday last year," I told my mother.

I REALLY did not want to wear that hat. But the look on my mother's face told me that I was going to wear it anyway. Funny how you can sometimes see into the future by looking into a parent's face.

Our entrees came. The good news is that pumpkin tortellini is my new favorite food. The bad news is that I discovered this while dressed as a doughnut salesman.

I lost myself in the pumpkiny goodness until Horse Ass got a phone call that broke my spell. My dad would never have taken a call during dinner. Especially not during my birthday dinner. But Horse Ass just doesn't get it. To him a birthday dinner is just something that interferes with business.

Suddenly Horse Ass's conversation got very loud. He was saying things like, "You people gave me your word!" and, "This is highly unprofessional!" and, "This is not the way Ice Dogs likes to do business." He sounded ridiculous. A man in his forties should never say the words *Ice Dogs.* It's just plain embarrassing.

So much so that by the hundred and thirty-seventh time, I had to look around the restaurant to make sure people weren't pointing at us and laughing.

The good news was that no one was.

The bad news was that seated at the next table was none other than Hailey Sherman. Fiona, Bliss, and Madison were with her, of course.

This unfortunate coincidence could not have come at a worse time. Just when I was trying to get Hailey to forget my existence, there she was, eating dinner with her friends, all cool and adult-like with no grown-ups in sight, and there I was having dinner with my *family!* Oh, the shame!

I sank down as low as possible into my chair, hoping that Hailey wouldn't notice me. Then I remembered what I had on my head. The same kind of hat Esther the cafeteria lady wears. The chances that Hailey didn't notice me were slim. And when my mother clinked her glass with a spoon to make this toast—"To Raisin, who's growing into a young woman before my eyes," the chances got even slimmer.

How uncouth! Why not make a toast: "To Raisin, whose bosoms are rounding out nicely and who should start getting her period within the year"?

Toast or no toast, I am not growing into a woman, and I have no intention of getting my period until the age of thirty at least. I wanted to give my mother a heads-up on this so that she'd hold off on any more toasts like that for another seventeen years. But she got up to go to the bathroom before I had a chance.

Without her around, everyone at the table seemed uncomfortable. Except for Lola, who was eating tiny pieces of rolled-up napkin. Actually Samantha, who was reading from the anthropology textbook she had hidden under the table, seemed pretty content too. Technically Samantha should have been paying attention to me, the birthday girl. But I'm so grateful that she hasn't mentioned the missing bra, she can do whatever she wants for all I care.

So I guess it was only me and Horse Ass who felt uncomfortable. We just kind of sat quietly exchanging grins for a while until he finally broke the ice.

"So, dude . . ." HA started. Yes, he calls me dude. Let's not overthink it, shall we?

"You got a boyfriend?"

"You got a boyfriend" he asks me! Blechhh . . . yuck . . . disgusting . . . vomitacious! No way would I discuss my love life with THAT MAN. I wouldn't even discuss it with my dad. And he's my dad! Not that Peter Rodriguez would ever try. He understands that fathers and daughters aren't supposed to discuss that kind of thing. Even last year, when I accidentally left the Valentine's Day card I got from Thomas in his car, he never said a word about it to me. Now, that's perfect father-daughter communication.

Finally my mom came back, saving me from having

to answer Horace. Unfortunately she brought bad news with her.

"I ran into that lovely Hailey in the bathroom and invited her and her friends to join us later for some birthday cake."

How could she? I wondered. Didn't she know I was on the run from Hailey? Which again begs the familiar question, Why is my mother out to get me?

Next thing I knew, the happy birthday song was coming from Hailey's table. Across the room, a waiter carried a piece of birthday cake out of the kitchen. I could hardly believe my eyes. *A birthday cake,* I wondered. *From Hailey?* Here I was thinking that Hailey never wanted a thing to do with me again, yet she was ordering birthday cake for me. What a nice thing for her to do. I must have misjudged. All along I thought she was turned off by the unseemliness of that nasty dog incident, while in truth she was able to tune it all out and see straight through to my unique brand of *je ne sais quoi.*

I sat frozen in my chair for a moment. But since none of the girls were getting up and the waiter had almost reached their table, I figured I was supposed to go for it myself.

As I headed toward them, I felt my face beam with pride. But I didn't want to beam! I wanted to appear nonchalant. Bored silly. As if this kind of thing happened to me every day. Still, my mouth was fighting me. It kept breaking into this stupid grin. The only way to stop it would have been to push the corners of my lips back in place. Which would not have looked nonchalant or bored. Just idiotic.

I arrived at their table as they were singing the final "happy birthday." And as they got to the end of the song, I stood there like an imbecile as they sang out "dear Fiona" instead of "dear Raisin."

That cake wasn't for me! That song wasn't for me! They didn't care that it was my birthday! So why was I standing there, glowing like Ms. America waiting to be crowned?

Everything began to move in slow motion. The room turned fuzzy and my face turned red-hot. I had to say something. "Isn't it funny that you and I have the same birthday?" might have worked. But it's hard to speak when you're using all your strength to fight back an ocean of tears.

Instead I chose to gloss over the whole incident. To act like I was just passing their table on the way to someplace else. And that there was no connection between their singing of the birthday song and the paper hat on my head with the words *Happy Birthday* scribbled along the side. So after loitering at their table for a good twelve seconds with my mouth wide open, I headed for the bar, as if that's where I was going all along.

I took a seat on the stool and waited for the bartender to take my order. If I could somehow manage to have them see me with a drink in hand, my pride could be salvaged.

Three minutes passed and the bartender still hadn't come over. Even though no one else was seated at the bar but me. I kept waiting and still nothing. Why wouldn't he serve me?

"What's a girl gotta do to get some service around here?"

He continued to ignore me in spite of my forceful tone. Now his behavior bordered on rude.

"Raisin, have you lost your mind?" my mother asked, sneaking up behind me.

"I'm sorry," I said turning toward her. I know how important proper language is to her, but I was having a crisis; couldn't she have let it slide? "What does a young woman need to do to acquire a drink around here?" I said to the bartender, correcting myself.

I turned back toward her. "Better?" I asked.

"Raisin, I have no idea what ridiculous game it is that you're playing, but get off that bar stool right now and join us back at the table."

I glanced over at the girls to make sure they didn't

hear my mother's inappropriate outburst. But my concern was unnecessary. They'd completely forgotten about me—lost in their own world of fabulosity and presents. Gag gifts—extra-strength deodorant . . . athlete's foot powder . . . a book called *Finding Love After Fifty*—just like the ones you guys sent me.

"All I wanted was to order a Shirley Temple," I answered, looking her dead in the eye.

"Order it at the table," she said, looking like she wanted me dead.

"What's wrong with wanting to knock one back in celebration of my thirteenth birthday?"

She almost knocked me out for that one.

When I got back to the table, there were gift boxes from Giselle's waiting for me. The plaid skirt, the brown velour sweat suit, the tank top, and the Adidas.

It was nice to be reunited with my rightful clothes, but I would have traded them all for a chance to erase those last ten minutes of embarrassment in a heartbeat. That or an invitation to join Fiona's birthday celebration.

Maybe next year. By then they'll have realized how fantastic I am. They'll wonder how they ever celebrated Fiona's birthday without me.

The only thing that made up for the awfulosity were the packages waiting for me when I got home. Yours and my dad's. He sent me this pair of red cowboy boots

I'd always wanted (which would go perfectly with a certain red leather bag) and an open plane ticket to Berkeley, which I plan to use very, very soon.

But the best part of it all was the pennies he put inside the envelope. He does that every year. Gives me one penny for every year I've been alive and an extra one for good luck. It's always been my favorite part of my birthday. I wasn't sure he'd remember. But he did, of course . . . because that's the kind of guy he is. I miss him.

Comments:

Logged in at 4:15 PM, EST

PiaBallerina: Rae-rae, I'm sorry your birthday dinner was so yucky. Maybe Hailey and her friends didn't even realize you thought the cake was for you. And if they did, I'm sure they'll forget about it.

Logged in at 4:27 PM, EST

kweenclaudia: i would just like to take the opportunity to point out that the presents we got you are much funnier than the presents fiona's friends got for her.

Thursday, September 30

7:05 AM, EST

Feline Friends,

Of course your presents were funnier, Claud. It's just that

those girls are . . . hereier. And maybe you're right. Maybe
the Fiona and Haileys didn't even realize I thought the cake
was for me. I'm going to try and feel out the situation.

12:33 PM, EST

That went really well.

On Planet Exactly the Opposite.

At the beginning of lunch I went up to their table and
said, "Hey, was that you guys at Antonio's last night?"

Madison and Bliss gave me a confused look. Fiona
didn't even bother lifting her eyes from her sandwich.

"Raisin, what are you talking about?" Hailey finally
replied. "Of course you saw us at Antonio's. You came
right up to our table after we sang the birthday song to
Fiona. I think you thought the cake was for you."

"Right," I said. "Just making sure . . ."

Why couldn't I have kept my mouth shut? Why can't
I control my talktoomucheosis? I should go live in a box.

But in the meantime, I think it's probably best for
me to spend the rest of the day in the bathroom of the
girls locker room.

I'm betting you guys do too. . . .

4:15 PM, EST

I finally found something I like about Franklin
Academy. You can cut class without getting caught! I

don't know why anyone bothers going to class at all. . . .

I spent the entire afternoon in one of the bathroom stalls of the girls locker room and ran into no trouble at all.

Plus I overheard a valuable bit of information.

The Fiona and Haileys made a stop in the bathroom before I had a chance to sneak out. I overheard Hailey talking about the soccer team. She's the captain, and she's worried that this year's team won't be as good as last year's team. But her friends told her not to worry. Tryouts are on Tuesday, and some good players are bound to show up.

I wonder if there's some way I could get involved?

7:25 PM, EST

I figured out why people go to class at Franklin Academy. Because if they don't, THE ATTENDANCE SUPERVISOR CALLS HOME, that's why.

Why do they have to be so sneaky about it? Why can't they just sniff you out and send you to the principal the way they do in Berkeley?

IT'S NOT FAIR!

My mom just got the call. Of course she picked this night out of all nights to come home in time for dinner. And here's the crazy part—*she's* angry with *me*.

"Raisin, it's only the third week of school and you're already cutting classes. And not just one class, but *three!* Do you have some sort of explanation for me?"

"Yes, I do, actually. The explanation is that it's all your fault. I've been trying and trying to make friends here, and whenever I come close, you come along and do everything you can to ruin it."

Then I stormed off to my bedroom and slammed the door behind me. Which will probably add years to my grounding sentence. My mom hates when I slam the door.

Wait . . .

She's coming up the stairs. . . .

This could get ugly. . . .

If you don't hear from me in the next day or two, alert the media.

Pia, you can have my wardrobe, and Claudia, you can have the Preparation H.

7:45 PM, EST

As I live and breathe! She's not punishing me. We just had a "talk" instead—the kind they have on those hour-long family dramas. Only different because neither of us has glow in the dark white teeth like the actresses who pretend to have those talks on TV.

"Raisin," she began as she stood in my doorway. "May I come in?"

"Sure," I said, hoping to make up for slamming the door by using an inviting tone.

"Can you tell me what I've done to ruin your chances at making friends?" Mom asked. She'd taken a seat at the edge of my bed and now she was petting my hair. I took this as a good sign.

"You *want* me to tell you what you've done to ruin my chances at making friends?" I was double checking just to make sure I understood her correctly. Wouldn't have wanted to get myself back into trouble.

She nodded.

"Well, you wouldn't let me keep sassy student. And you put me in charge of walking Countess. And then to top it off, you invited Hailey to have birthday cake with us!"

I hoped I wasn't being *too* brutal. But she did say she wanted the truth.

"Raisin, honey. I'm not sure I followed all that," she started. "But I'm genuinely sorry for whatever I've done."

That seemed like a promising response. . . .

"So you're not going to ground me?" By then I was bouncing up and down on the bed and throwing my arms around her neck.

"No," she answered in a tone that meant, "Stop bouncing or I might."

"That wouldn't solve anything," she continued. "More than anything I want you to be happy and to make friends. And like I said the night I sent you to Giselle's, one of the best ways for you to make that happen is by joining some after-school activities. Do you think that's something you'd like to try?"

"Yeah, Mom. I'll try."

Then she hugged me and left the room.

. . . Phew! That was close.

I'm glad she didn't ground me. But I still haven't forgotten that this whole thing is her fault.

I wonder which after-school activity I should join?

Comments:

Logged in at 8:15 PM, EST

PiaBallerina: **Weren't you just saying that Hailey's looking for new players to join the soccer team?**

Logged in at 8:22 PM, EST

kweenclaudia: **how come I get the preparation h?**

8:54 PM, EST

Sorry, Claud, I thought you'd be psyched about it. Think of the many uses!

And Pi, are you suggesting that I join the soccer team? I guess I could. . . .

Though to be honest, I've never really been sure what the fuss is all about. If I remember correctly, no one tells any jokes. There are no glittery outfits. No snacks are served. But there must be something to it because Hailey seems to take it really seriously.

Comments:

Logged in 8:15 PM, EST

<u>PiaBallerina</u>: You should just give it a try, Rae. You might like it too.

Logged in at 8:17 PM, EST

<u>kweenclaudia</u>: pia, i don't know if that's such a good idea.

Logged in at 8:23 PM, EST

<u>PiaBallerina</u>: Claudia! Why are you saying that?

Logged in at 8:26 PM, EST

<u>kweenclaudia</u>: what? i'm turning over a new leaf. trying to be nicer from now on and make sure rae leaves me something better than preparation h.

Logged in at 8:35 PM, EST

<u>PiaBallerina</u>: How is that nice?

Logged in at 8:47 PM, EST

<u>kweenclaudia</u>: have you ever see raisin play sports?

Logged in at 8:53 PM, EST

<u>PiaBallerina</u>: I know, but if the team at her school is anything like our team, they'll let anyone join.

9:03 PM, EST

Hel-lo-oo! I'm here! I can see your nasty little comments!

But I'm willing to let you guys make it up to me! All you have to do is write out instructions on how to play.

Comments:

Logged in at 9:55 PM, EST

<u>PiaBallerina</u>: Ask Jeremy.

Logged in at 9:56 PM, EST

<u>kweenclaudia</u>: what she said.

Friday, October 1

7:03 PM, EST

Kitties,

I think I will ask Jeremy. If his jumping-over-gates and sweat-hockey skills are any indication, he's probably really good at sports.

4:54 PM, EST

I took your advice. On the way home from school I asked Jeremy to teach me how to play soccer.

"I would if I didn't have so much homework," he said, pointing to his full backpack.

"But it's Friday," I reminded him.

"So?" he asked.

"So, you have all weekend to do your homework," I reminded him. Sometimes he can be such a space cadet.

"Well, I want to pace myself," he said.

"You're planning on spending the whole weekend doing homework?" I asked.

"Look, Raisin, it's nothing personal, but teaching a girl how to play soccer seems kind of boring," he finally said. Who knew Jeremy could be so harsh?

"Okay, Jeremy. Listen. I saw the way you looked at Fiona during lunch the other day—"

"I did not look at Fiona the other day—" he protested. Right . . . that's why his face was getting so red it was turning into one giant freckle.

"Okay, fine. You didn't look at Fiona. All I'm saying is, she's on the soccer team—"

"She's a *starter* on the soccer team," he said, correcting me.

"Fine. Even better. If she's a starter and I'm on the team, and she and I get to be friends, and you and I are friends, then the three of us can hang out together . . . bada bing, bada boom. Ya follow me?"

"I guess so. All right. I'll teach you. Monday after school. My place."

Men. Can't live with 'em. Can't get them to teach

you how to play soccer without promising to hook them up with the seventh-grade sex goddess who doesn't even know your name.

Comments:

Logged in at 9:34 PM, EST

PiaBallerina: That's great, Rae! Oh yeah—you were right about Danny—he does get potato chips caught in his braces.

Logged in at 9:37 PM, EST

kweenclaudia: tell raisin how you know. . . .

Logged in at 9:42 PM, EST

PiaBallerina: Because I kissed him.

Logged in at 9:46 PM, EST

kweenclaudia: tell her for how long.

Logged in at 9:49 PM, EST

PiaBallerina: Six seconds!

Logged in at 9:52 PM, EST

kweenclaudia: tell her where.

Logged in at 9:55 PM, EST

PiaBallerina: Behind the bleachers on the softball field.

Logged in at 9:53 PM, EST

<u>kweenclaudia</u>: that's right, rae. our little girl's growing up. now I've gotta get me a man!

Monday, October 4

7:06 AM, EST

Kitty Cats,

Pi! I'm so excited! We're going to be cousins-in-law!

12:43 PM, EST

CJ brought a rolled-up Armani shopping bag to class. Whatever he had in it seemed very big and heavy. I was so curious, I had to ask him what it was.

"Hey, CJ, what's in the bag?" I whispered to him when the teacher had his back turned.

But CJ didn't say anything. He didn't even look up from his drawing, so I asked him again in case he didn't hear me.

"Uh, my lunch," he answered, his head still in his drawing.

I knew he had to be making that up. Unless there was a brontosaurus burger in that bag, there's no way it was his lunch.

He talked to me, though. Which I guess is progress. Until now I thought he only communicated with the guy in the drawing.

I looked for CJ during lunch to see what he was eating. It most definitely was not a brontosaurus burger. More like a tuna sandwich. And he was sitting with this alt boy who has green hair who was doing all the talking. To be fair, CJ was doing all the nodding.

He's such a mystery, that CJ. A non-speaking, cinnamon-scented, mysterious-bag-carrying mystery!

7:11 PM, EST

(Seven-eleven . . . HA! Speaking of which . . . They don't have 7-Elevens here. They have the Wawa. The Wawa! Can you imagine? Great name . . . wonder who came up with it . . . Helen Keller . . . HA! Helen Keller! Haven't told a good Helen Keller joke in years!)

But I digress. . . .

Went to Jeremy's house so he could teach me how to play soccer. He explained the rules to me. Then we kicked the ball around for about an hour.

Turns out I'm a remarkably quick study. I got twelve goals. Jeremy kept insisting my goals didn't count because I used my hands.

"But it's so much easier when you use your hands," I said. I think this made him very angry. I could tell because he slammed the ball against the side of his house and yelled, "There's only one rule in soccer—you can't use your hands!" He repeated the part about not using your hands like five times.

It can't be healthy to get so angry, so I told Jeremy we didn't need to practice anymore. What difference does it make if he's right about the hands rule or not? It's only a game. It's not like I'm going for an Olympic medal. I just want a chance to hang out with Fiona and her friends.

"Don't even worry about it," Jeremy said. "You're gonna be fine. The soccer team pretty much takes anyone who tries out. They pretend there's an elimination process, but everyone knows it's a scam."

Just like at Berkeley. Still, I wish he could have told me that before our practice. That's an hour of my life I'll never get back.

"So, if I just ran around the field a lot without going near the ball, do you think I'd get busted?" I asked.

"Maybe not right away."

"That's good enough for me," I said. "What's for dinner?"

Comments:

Logged in at 8:36 PM, EST

kweenclaudia: you should say you were the star sweeper at berkeley middle school. that's the perfect position for you.

8:43 PM, EST

A sweeper? Me? Thanks for the advice, Claud. You're

too kind. Really . . . But I'm not sure being the team maid will garner me the kind of respect I'm looking for.

PS—What happened to trying to say nice things?

Comments:

Logged in at 8:51 PM, EST

<u>PiaBallerina</u>: Raisin, you don't understand. . . . The sweeper is a position on a soccer team. She's the person who covers the areas between the fullbacks and the goals. It's a perfect position for you because the sweeper can run around and uh, you know . . . pretend to be doing stuff without really doing anything.

9:25 PM, EST

Sorry so snappish, Claud . . . Sometimes it's easy to misunderstand people in cyberspace. I wish you guys were here so that we could misunderstand each other in person. Anyway, wish me luck. Tryouts are tomorrow.

Tuesday, October 5

9:27 PM, EST

I made the team! I made the team! Yippee for me, I made the team!

All I had to do was kick the ball when the coach rolled it to me. I even played Jeremy's way and didn't use my hands once. I can't believe that's all I had to do. It's a wonder they can keep out the slackers.

Uccch! Guess who's at my door again, begging to be taken out for a walk. I'll give you a hint: it's the Michael Jackson of the pet world.

Well, my punishment is over. Countess is not my responsibility anymore. I'm going to march right into Samantha's room and tell her to take her nose out of whatever book she's reading and walk her dog.

9:35 PM, EST

I finally figured out why Samantha's always on the phone!

I was bringing Countess over to her room through our adjoining bathroom. Sam usually keeps her door tightly shut and I always knock first before entering. But this time it must have been slightly ajar because Countess went barreling right through it, and when the door opened, guess what I saw? Samantha with a *boy* on her bed! And you'll never guess what they were doing . . .

They were MAKING OUT! Like in-the-movies making out. Smoochy noises and everything. I mean, they were practically swallowing each other's faces!!

As soon as Samantha noticed me, she pulled away from him. Part of me was grateful because watching someone you know going at it is a very strange experience. But another teeny tiny part of me wanted to watch for longer. I guess I never thought of Samantha as someone who kisses boys. Or even thinks about them.

"Oh, hi, Raisin," Samantha said as she adjusted her ponytail. "This is my friend Sid. . . ."

I must say, Sid, whose hair was gelled into a rat's nest and who wore low-slung flared jeans with a track jacket on top, seemed a little hip for Samantha.

"Nice to meet you," I said, walking toward him to shake his hand. But Samantha got right up off the bed and redirected me to the bathroom. Then she closed the door behind us.

"It's not my fault," I said before she had a chance to yell at me for forgetting to knock.

"It's okay, Raisin, I'm not mad. Just promise me you won't tell anyone about him. Not my dad. Not your mom. No one. I'd be dead if anyone found out about him. Promise?"

"Sure, Sam," I said.

"Swear?"

"I swear."

"I really appreciate it," she said, hugging me. "You're the best. And as a thank-you, feel free to borrow any of my clothes."

Easy for her to say. She's twice my height. Now, if she'd offered to let me borrow her hair, that might have been worth something to me.

I closed the door behind me, wondering why Sid had to be a secret. I mean, Sam's sixteen. She must be allowed to date boys.

Just then I heard them whispering about something. I figured it had to be important, so I put my ear up to the wall to listen.

"That's why we should always hang out in my dorm room," I heard Sid say.

Dorm room! You know what that means! Sid's a college student. Which explains why Sam's keeping him a secret.

"I know, it's just that we have no privacy there," Sam said back.

Privacy! You know what that means! That means Sam wants to do dirty things with her boyfriend. I've never seen anyone go so quickly from boringly bookish to fascinatingly fascinating in my life! I think I'm starting to like that girl!

I wanted to stay in the bathroom and keep eavesdropping. But Countess kept whimpering and I didn't want to get caught listening. Besides, he could have an accident. Last time I made him wait, he peed on Lola's Barbie. Then Lola flushed the doll down my toilet and when it overflowed, *I* was the one who got in trouble for it.

Gotta go!

PS—I forgot to tell you who the soccer coach is . . . Ferguson! The earth-science teacher I told you about with the unfortunate body-hair placement. Wait! Make that FURguson! Ha! Good one! Can't wait to share it with the girls.

Comments:

Logged in at 7:10 PM, EST

<u>kweenclaudia</u>: it's always the librarians, isn't it?

Logged in at 7:15 PM, EST

<u>PiaBallerina</u>: Congratulations on making the soccer team! I saw your dad today when I met my mom at his yoga studio. If I had known, I would have told him.

Wednesday, October 6

7:06 AM, EST

Kitties,

You saw my dad, Pi?

At his studio?

I wish I had seen him.

What color was his aura?

Were his chakras clean?

You know, the answer is within.

7:09 AM, EST

How's he holdin' up without me?

12:32 PM, EST

You know what I forgot to think about?

I forgot to think about the fact that I'm going to be playing soccer with the Fiona and Haileys. Sure, that was the whole point of trying out, but those guys think I'm a weirdo!

Well, if I stop acting like a weirdo, then maybe they'll stop thinking I'm one.

5:43 PM, EST

Just got back from my first soccer practice. I tried very hard not to act like a weirdo, which is probably why no one treated me like one. But no one treated me like her new best friend forever, either.

When I got to the locker room, Fiona, Madison, and Bliss were already there. Fiona was checking out her uniform in the mirror. Or uniforms, to be more accurate. She bought two. One for fat days and one for skinny ones. I suppose that level of preparation makes sense for her. She's a sex goddess. She has her public to think about.

I, on the other hand, did not need a skinny uniform. Or a fat uniform, for that matter. I needed a *different* uniform. Let's face it, ladies, the T-shirt tucked into the elasticized waistband shorts is a tough look to pull off. And the sweat socks pulled all the way up to the knees don't do much to help it.

Just as I was checking myself out in the mirror, Hailey

burst into the room and started crying about Mike Leary.

"He's always flirting with other seventh-grade girls," she said. I could have cried too. That uniform made me look REE-TARDED.

"I caught him flirting by the second-floor soda machine," Hailey continued. "With one of those alt girls, of all people!"

Madison got up off the bench to hug her and Bliss went to get her a tissue. Fiona gave her a pouty face and blew a kiss in her direction before going back to her reflection. "Don't worry," Madison said. "You're the one he asked out."

"You should tell him to stop," Bliss added. "If he doesn't, he's a jerk and who needs him anyway."

I felt like I should say something. If I wanted to be one of them, it seemed like I should start contributing. But what could I say? I don't have much experience dating flirts.

. . . Guess I'm one of the lucky ones.

"Yeah, who needs him?" I finally added. Sure, I was just repeating what Bliss had already said, but at least I was following.

The girls didn't seem to appreciate my comment at all. They each just threw me a quick "I don't appreciate your comment at all" look and went back to their powwow.

As soon as practice started, I could tell that everyone else on the team played a lot better than I do. They ran faster, kicked harder . . . knew the rules.

I realized that the smartest thing I could do was to stay as far away from the ball as possible. That way I could avoid dropping the ball or kicking it past the wrong goal. Unfortunately it also meant never scoring points for the team.

I've noticed that scoring points for the team is a good way to get people to like you. They high-five you. Even hug you. And after practice they talk to you. They might begin by saying something soccer-related like, "Nice score." But it often evolves into something personal like, "What color lip gloss are you wearing?"

No one said anything to me after practice. Not even, "I like how you stayed away from the ball."

I'm not really sure about this whole soccer thing.

Comments:

Logged in at 7:46 PM, EST

PiaBallerina: Maybe you shouldn't feel like you have to avoid the ball. . . . Maybe you're not as bad as you think?

PS—Your dad looked like he's holding up well. But like he misses you.

Logged in at 7:54 PM, EST

kweenclaudia: maybe i found a boyfriend.

Logged in at 7:57 PM, EST
   <u>PiaBallerina</u>: Claudia! Why didn't you tell me? Who is it?

Logged in at 8:03 PM, EST
   <u>kweenclaudia</u>: i wanted to tell you both at once. it's my paperboy!

Logged in at 8:06 PM, EST
   <u>kweenclaudia</u>: unless it's the boy who always sits on the mailbox at the end of my block.

Logged in at 8:11 PM, EST
   <u>PiaBallerina</u>: Who do you like better?

Logged in at 8:17 PM, EST
   <u>kweenclaudia</u>: tough to say. the paperboy is really sweet and friendly. but the boy who sits on the mailbox has two chipped teeth and he's kind of scary. so they each have something good going for them.

Logged in at 8:21 PM, EST
   <u>PiaBallerina</u>: I'd go for the paperboy.

Thursday, October 7

7:04 AM, EST
   Meow, meow,
      But the mailbox boy sounds more like Claudia's type. Don't ya think?

6:25 PM, EST

Still avoiding the ball during scrimmages. Believe it or not, this is hard work and can get very exhausting. I think it's all the trembling I do whenever the ball comes near me.

It's a wonder no one's noticed yet. Either I'm a really good faker, or I've already been booted off the team and someone's forgotten to tell me.

Which wouldn't surprise me since no one talks to me. I might as well go back to pulling bras out of dogs' butts and wearing stupid Krispy Kreme hats because nothing I do seems to make a difference.

On a more positive note, I came *thisclose* to finding out what CJ keeps in the bag. It was sheer brilliance on my part. I noticed in math today that his bag wasn't rolled shut the way it usually is. So after the teacher assigned an in-class problem, I seized the opportunity and dropped my pencil inside. My plan was to have a look as I retrieved the pencil. But just as I reached into the bag and got a whiff of that cinnamony goodness, CJ dove in and got it out himself.

"I think you dropped this," he said, handing me the pencil. He was almost looking at me, but not quite. I was able to get a partial glimpse of his face, though. Definitely very good looking. Though I still won't know whether he's gorgeous until I find out what's in the bag.

When it comes to boys, it's not just about the face for me. It's about the whole package.

I wish he would just tell me what's in the bag!

What could it be??? Maybe it's his fortune in gold, or an antique record collection, or some rare animal skull. . . .

Comments:

Logged in at 7:52 PM, EST
kweenclaudia: maybe it's his dirty laundry. . . .

Logged in at 7:57 PM, EST
PiaBallerina: Have you picked one of the boys yet, Claud?

Logged in at 7:59 PM, EST
kweenclaudia: not yet. i'm really torn. the paperboy and i have a lot in common. we both like watching baseball and reading comics, and we both want to be lawyers when we grow up. but the mailbox boy wears a tiny hoop nose ring, which makes him look tough yet oddly girly.

Friday, October 8

7:07 AM, EST
Dear Kitty, Kitty,
    Mailbox boy sounds dreamy. . . .

6:48 PM, EST
    Fiona: Raina, have you ever played soccer before?
    Raisin: Of course I have. Why? Would you like some pointers?

Fiona (*ignoring that last question*): Then why are you always running away from the ball? As sweeper you're supposed to make sure everyone's covered.

Raisin (*pretending she has a clue*): Really? You want me to make sure everyone's covered? That's not exactly how we do it in Berkeley, but sure, Fi. If that's what you want, I'll make sure everyone's cov—

Fiona (*interrupting*): Glad to hear it. And Raina? Please don't call me Fi.

Monday, October 11

5:26 PM, EST

Hello Kitties,

I, Raisin Rodriguez, expert at large, math genius, and close personal friend to Madonna, have a new talent to add to my repertoire. Scorer of soccer goals.

Thank you, thank you, it's truly an honor just to be nominated.

It was nothing, really.

Anyone could have done it.

Dumb luck, as they say.

Okay, fine, it was a complete accident. . . .

But who's keeping score?

It all started when I went to grab a soda from the second-floor machine during homeroom today. I was searching for one last quarter when a hand appeared out of nowhere, holding one. The hand, of course, belonged to Sparkles.

"New Girl, what's up with your bangs?" he asked, sounding deeply concerned. Which is kind of strange considering I cut my bangs three weeks ago.

"I, uh . . ."

"Don't worry. We don't have to go there. But while you're waiting for them to grow in, try shampooing with aspirin. It'll make your hair so shiny, the bangs will be less noticeable."

I couldn't wait to go home and try it.

Later, during scrimmages, Bliss kicked the ball to me. Normally when this happens, as you know, I like to wave my hands in the air and run in the opposite direction. But this time when the ball came at me, I wasn't even paying attention. I was too preoccupied by what Sparkles had told me.

I wondered what it was about the aspirin . . . the acid burning away the outer layer of the hair shaft? Or the medicinal quality that makes hair, just like people, feel better after taking it?

As I considered the different possibilities, I got lost in thought. Too lost to notice the ball or react to it in any way. Which was great because instead of messing things up by getting involved, I just stood still as the ball bounced off my head and straight past the other team's goalie. And just my luck, it was the winning goal!

As we cleared the court, lots of people congratulated me. Patted me on the back. Some punched me on the arm. I was in such a good mood, I didn't even punch anyone back.

I don't want to jump to any conclusions, but I think even Hailey was impressed. She came up to me in the locker room and said, "Raisin, I'm impressed."

And get this—I think Fiona was too. She happened to be standing next to Hailey and said to me, "Me too."

It was nice to hear. Still, I was hoping these comments would lead to more of a conversation. Maybe a question about what color lip gloss I was wearing. Or, since I wasn't wearing any lip gloss, a conversation about when I was free for a sleepover . . .

But I guess there's plenty of time for that.

As we changed, the coach announced the starting team for game one, which is tomorrow. And believe it or not, yours truly was on that list! Must have been some goal I made!

I've got to say, these last few hours have been such a thrill ride. It's like my life has done a complete hundred-and-eighty-degree turn. Fiona and Hailey are suddenly talking to me. I'll be able to make good on my promise to Jeremy. And after tonight's shampoo my hair will be shinier. Maybe my mom was right about getting involved with after-school activities. . . .

But I won't lie to you guys. There are times when I miss my privacy. There are moments when I wish I could step out the door without having to worry about being photographed or followed. I shouldn't complain. These concerns are the small price you pay for doing the thing you love and doing it well.

Comments:

Logged in at 8:03 PM, EST

<u>PiaBallerina</u>: That's great, Rae. I'm really happy for you. I wish my life were going as well as yours.

Logged in at 8:07 PM, EST

<u>kweenclaudia</u>: your stupid cousin broke up with pia today. he said he has to save his energy for jujitsu.

but congratulations on your good news! here's to a hard head!

9:03 PM, EST

I'm so sorry, Pi. I forgot about how crazy Danny gets over jujitsu. He's the one with the hard head. But you can do sooo much better than him. Someone who doesn't get potato chips stuck in his braces. Maybe someone who doesn't eat potato chips at all . . .

Tuesday, October 12

12:33 PM, EST

Dear Kitten and Cat,

Fiona and Hailey have been so nice to me all day. During math Hailey passed me a note. And not to give to Fiona either. It said, *I hope you're ready for the game.* Not exactly, *Come over after school for an evening of beauty. Maybe you can tell us how you got your hair so shiny . . .* but definitely an improvement over the sneers I used to get from her. Then at lunch Fiona walked by my table and said, "Hey, Rachel, make sure you load up on carbs."

When she left, Jeremy asked, "When are you going to let me start hanging out with you guys like you promised?"

Of course he said it loud enough for Fiona to hear. Sort of defeats the purpose of having me act as the middleman.

"Call me crazy," I told him, "but she just called me Rachel. I'm thinking of waiting until she learns my name before I try and interfere with her love life."

Men. Can't live with 'em. Can't get away with making impossible promises to set them up with seventh-grade sex goddesses.

"Well, you better not waste too much more time," he said.

Talk about hot to trot. If it were me, I'd wait until all those freckles cleared before putting the moves on the love of my life.

"Why, what's the rush?" I asked.

"You're playing Chestnut Hill Prep today, right?"

I didn't get the connection. No matter who we played, it wouldn't make his freckles fade any faster.

"Those girls are enormous. If you don't know what you're doing, they're liable to clobber you. Especially someone your size. And then you'll never have an in with Fiona."

I resented the implication. Obviously Jeremy hadn't heard about my brilliant goal yesterday.

"I'll have you know, I scored the winning goal in scrimmage yesterday."

"Whatever, Raisin. Just be careful."

I'll show him.

3:12 PM, EST

Actually, I won't.

Jeremy was right.

I had earth science last period today and after it was over, I asked Fiona and Hailey if it was true that the girls on the Chestnut Hill Prep team were big.

"Ginormous," they answered in unison.

"How can an entire team of girls be ginormous? Aren't any of them just plain large?"

"It's not just the soccer team; it's the whole school," Hailey answered.

"Why are they like that?"

"They say it's the milk their school serves in the cafeteria," Fiona explained.

"I heard it's because they're all cousins in a family of giants," Hailey countered.

Why didn't anyone warn me yesterday? What am I going to do? Those milk monsters are going to trounce me. Any ball they kick my way isn't bouncing off my head without taking the rest of me with it. I can't let Fiona and Hailey figure out I'm a fraud. Not now when they're finally starting to like me.

I have two choices:

1. Gain fifty pounds by five o'clock.

Pros: Getting to eat as much Chunky Monkey ice cream and as many bags of Sour Patch Kids as I can scarf down in two hours' time.

Cons: It could take years to get back my girlish figure.

2. Get out of playing the game.

Pros: Getting out of playing the game.

Cons: Never having the satisfaction of knowing I gave it my best.

I'm going with two. The satisfaction in knowing I gave it my best isn't nearly as satisfying as the satisfaction in knowing I didn't blow it with the Fiona and Haileys.

8:05 PM, EST

You guys should have seen me. I was positively a genius, if I do say so myself. . . .

It came to me in a flash. I was heading toward the gym, still with no excuse in mind. I couldn't get away with saying I wasn't feeling well. Ferguson had just seen me in earth science, where I looked fine . . . or even . . . dare I say . . . radiant. (It's the aspirin, I'm telling you!)

I considered admitting the truth. That when it came to soccer, I had no idea what I was doing. That the only reason I scored yesterday was because I was thinking about hair-care tips.

But I wasn't ready to go back to the simple life.

I considered admitting that I only joined the team to make friends with Hailey and Fiona. But I didn't want to sound too pathetic.

Not that either of these excuses would have worked on Ferguson. He'd grown to depend on me as his star sweeper. He wasn't about to let me go so easily.

I was halfway down the stairs that lead to the soccer field when it hit me. I couldn't *tell* Ferguson I was sick, but if I *showed* him I was sick, he'd have to let me out of the game.

The stairs that lead to the soccer field also lead to the cafeteria. The key to my scheme was tucked away in the basement of Franklin Academy. In the kitchen storage space. Under the watchful eye of Esther. Who was no doubt opening cans of mushroom soup for tomorrow's tuna casserole.

All I needed to do was weasel one of those cans away from her and I was home free.

"Hi, Esther," I said, walking through the kitchen's swinging doors. "How's it going?"

I was right on the money! There was Esther standing behind a counter, busy opening cans of soup. Too busy, it appeared, to stop and answer my question.

Time to turn on the Raisin charm, I figured.

"Nice . . . uh . . . nice . . . hairnet, Esther," I offered.

"Who are you?" she asked in her Count Chocula accent. When she said the *h* sound, it came out like she was clearing her throat.

"My name is Raisin. I'm on the soccer team."

"You student. You not supposed to be een here," she said. Her prickly manner didn't deter me. I know her kind. All rough edges on the outside. Pure mush on the inside.

"Oh, I'm sorry, it just smelled so good, I had to come in here and see what you were making." There was no way I could lose with more compliments.

"Tuna casserole. I serve two times every week. Nobody like eet and I don't care. Vat you vant from me?"

She sure wasn't making it easy. I had no choice but to play up my weakness.

"Actually, would it be too much trouble to ask you for the recipe?"

"Eet's on side of can. Go ayvay, I'm busy."

I was losing ground. It was time to pull out all the stops.

"Well, do you mind if I copy it down? I'm a close personal friend of Madonna."

Her eyes widened. Clearly she hadn't realized who she was dealing with. "You are veird kid, no?" she asked.

"No, I'm just new here and I don't have many friends."

"Sorry. I very busy." Poor thing must have misunderstood me. I was asking her for a recipe, not a date.

"I just want to share your recipe with my mother. So she can make it at home." I hoped that would set her straight.

"Fine. Do your beezniss and get out."

Finally we were getting somewhere. With her back toward me, I found an open can and poured some soup into an old foam cup that was lying around.

So far, so good.

I got to the field. Just as I had hoped, no one was there but Ferguson, dusting off the bleachers.

Time to get the show on the road.

I'll admit to a little nervousness on my part. I'd never done anything like what I was about to do.

I made sure that no one but Ferguson was around and that he'd have his back toward me long enough for me to complete the deed. Then I coughed as loud as I could, made a retching noise (which made me gag and almost throw up for real), and spilled some of the soup on the ground.

"Raisin, are you all right?" he asked.

I knitted my eyebrows and looked at the ground.

"Do you think I can still play?" I asked, in my most disappointed-sounding voice.

Just then Madison came out of the locker room to see what was going on. When she saw what was on the ground, she said, "Ewww, gross. It looks like mushroom soup." Then she turned green and threw up for real.

Ferguson looked on the verge of throwing up himself and told us we should both go home. Madison went to call her mom. I said my parents were both working, so Ferguson asked Madison if she could drop me off at home.

In the car Madison cried because she wanted to play so badly.

"Don't cry, Madison," I told her. "We have the whole season to play."

"I know. I'm just worried that without both of us playing, our team might lose."

I guess that should have made me feel bad, but in a way it made me feel good. Madison really considered me important to the team.

When I got home, I crawled into bed and played sick for the rest of the night. Then my mom came home and asked me why I wasn't at soccer. I told her I threw up, which made her cry too.

"I'm sorry you're having such a tough time of it, Raisin. But I'm really proud of you for trying."

I didn't mean to make my mom cry. Or to make Madison throw up. I guess mushroom soup just has that effect on people.

Comments:

Logged in at 9:14 PM, EST

<u>PiaBallerina</u>: Rae . . . I'm speechless.

Logged in at 9:09 PM, EST

<u>kweenclaudia</u>: nice job! couldn't have done it better myself. btw, mailbox boy is out. when i passed him today, his nose ring was on the other nostril. turns out there's no piercing. it's just a magnet. obviously, it could never work.

Wednesday, October 13

12:16 PM, EST

Kitties!

You'll never ever, ever, ever, guess who called me. Fiona Small!

That's right . . . Fiona Fionarita Small!

The one and only Fiona Fionestra Smallen Small!

I was on the phone with my dad, telling him all about making the soccer team. The girls on the team . . . what a sweeper does . . . how great it is that I have a really hard head. And he was saying how proud he was of me. That when I visit, we can kick around a ball in his backyard. I think he might even tell Madonna about me. Then call waiting beeped in. And when I picked up, it was Fiona!

"Hi, is this Raisin?" she asked.

"Yes," I answered.

"Hi, Raisin, this is Fiona. How are you feeling?"

"Fine, and you?" I answered, forgetting that I was supposed to have been really sick earlier in the day. I think I was thrown by the fact that she called me by my correct name. Twice.

"I meant . . . I'm feeling better. How'd the game go?"

"Not well. We lost. Which is why I'm calling."

I panicked. Did she blame the team's loss on my absence? Or worse, did Esther rat me out?

"You still there?" she asked.

"Yeah, sorry."

"Anyway, I just wanted to make sure that you were feeling better and that you'd be at the game on Thursday. It's against Merion, our biggest rival, so we're really going to need you."

"I'll definitely be there."

"Great. See you then," she said, and hung up.

Pretty normal conversation, right? No reason for me to worry or think she knows anything, right?

Comments:

Logged in at 5:11 PM, EST

<u>PiaBallerina</u>: Yeah. Seems pretty normal to me.

5:43 PM, EST

What do you mean, "Seems pretty normal"? That doesn't sound very convincing.

5:55 PM, EST

If you thought it was normal, you would just have said, "Sounds normal."

6:01 PM, EST

But you said "pretty normal," and "pretty" anything usually means "not quite" that thing.

6:17 PM, EST

If you think she knows, you should tell me. Honest. I can handle it.

6:53 PM, EST

For the love of Pete, tell me. Please.

Comments:

Logged in at 7:10 PM, EST

<u>PiaBallerina</u>: Rae, relax. I only said "pretty normal" because you said "pretty normal." Honest. I'm sure Fiona has no idea about the soup.

7:31 PM, EST

Okay. Thanks. I feel better.

Oh God! I never switched back to my dad after Fiona's call!

Better give him a call.

Thursday, October 14

12:03 PM, EST

Horror of horrors. It's all over. My life is over. My youth has passed me by. Everything has changed. Nothing will ever be the same. Especially on the fourteenth day of every month, when I'll be riddled with cramps, afraid to go swimming, reluctant to wear white, and just plain nasty to anyone who so much as looks at me without permission.

And as usual, there's only one person to blame.

That's right, folks. My mother must have put a curse on me when she made that awful toast at my birthday about me "growing into a young woman right before [her] . . . eyes."

Because all of a sudden and completely without warning, I GOT MY PERIOD!

I am no longer a carefree girl enjoying life without a worry in the world.

I am now a woman with a laundry list of concerns:

1. Tampon or sanitary pad?
2. Scented or unscented?
3. Small, medium, or large?
4. With wings or without? (And while we're on the subject . . . what's a sanitary pad doing with wings? Because if there's a chance of it flying off somewhere, it better not be on my time.)

And perhaps the most compelling question of all:

5. Why me?

I mean, let's be honest here. I don't think any of us were expecting it to happen to me first. I'm not equipped to handle something this big on my own. I mean, who do I have as a role model here—that Margaret girl?

She was no role model.

She had it all wrong. She couldn't wait to get hers. So much so, she asked God himself to speed up the process. Which is a complete waste of an opportunity if you ask me. If I had a direct line to God, I'd make proper use of it and ask him to take mine back.

And the timing couldn't be any worse. Today's the big soccer game. There's no way I'll get out of playing again. I have to try and give it my best shot, or all the progress I've made with the Fiona and Haileys will have been for nothing.

I guess I better go to the nurse and get something to stop up the leak.

12:25 PM, EST

Jeremy was in the nurse's office when I got there, so I left.

He's definitely starting to grow on me and everything, but there are certain situations where he's not to be trusted. I had visions of him saying something out loud in front of everyone, like, "What are you here for, a tampon or something?"

6:55 PM, EST

If only I *did* have a direct line to God, maybe things would be going better. Maybe he would take pity on me and not schedule my first period ever on the same day as my make-or-break soccer game. Or maybe he'd tell me how to stop screwing up and ruining all my chances at making friends. Or at least know what to say to make me feel better after I did.

It was so awful. . . . I had no luck in finding "feminine protection" as they call it. Not that I asked anyone. That would have been too embarrasing.

So I went to the game with a rolled-up tissue shoved in my underwear. Considering I had to keep my legs clamped together throughout the game to make sure nothing fell through my shorts, I was doing pretty well for myself. Managed not to go anywhere near the ball . . .

Until . . .

"Raisin, look over there!" I heard Hailey yell. I looked over to where I thought she was pointing and noticed a crumpled piece of something white on the ground. It looked suspiciously like the piece of tissue I had stuffed in my underwear.

My life at Franklin Academy flashed before my eyes. Of all the embarrassments and poomiliations I had suffered so far, that piece of tissue had rolled up inside of it the worst humiliation imaginable.

As I flew down the field to scoop it up before anyone else noticed it, I thought about how nice Hailey was to look out for me. But when I bent down to pick it up, it wasn't what I thought it was. Just a piece of white cloth. Unfortunately, as I was inspecting it, the soccer ball hit me on the head again.

But this time it didn't land in the other team's goal. This time it just fell to the ground, where someone from Merion got to it and kicked it right past our goalie, scoring the winning goal for her team.

As the Merion half of the spectators' stand went wild, the Fiona and Haileys huddled together in a group hug to console one another. I went to go join the huddle as well. After all, it was my loss too. But no one made room for me to get in. In fact, they edged me out.

It was so unfair. I wasn't the only one to blame for losing. If we hadn't been lagging behind in the first place, that one goal wouldn't have mattered.

Where was everyone's team spirit?

In any case, my being on the soccer team wasn't helping my cause one bit. I had to quit right away before I made the Fiona and Haileys hate me even more.

So I found Ferguson in the equipment shed and broke it to him gently.

"Mr. Ferguson," I started, "please don't take it personally, but I'm quitting the soccer team. I'm just no good."

"Raisin, have you given—"

"Yes," I said, interrupting him. "I've given it plenty of thought. And I know that as the coach, it's your job to try and talk me out of it. But it's no use."

"I was going to ask if you've given your uniform back to the manager."

Jeez, even the paid professionals won't pretend to care about me.

When I handed the uniform back to the manager, I felt like I was giving away my only chance. It was really hard to let go of it. In fact, he kind of had to grab the shorts out of my clutch. It's like they were the key to my only chance.

On my way out from school, I saw the Fiona and Haileys piling into Madison's mom's car. Fine, let them go have their giant group hug followed by the world's largest laugh-at-Raisinfest followed by celebratory brownie sundaes without me. Who needs 'em?

Not me, I tell ya.

Not me at all.

I'm fine all by myself. Me and my period-getting, bad-soccer-playing, can't-even-find-a-sanitary-pad-anywhere loser self.

PS—I wish Samantha would come home already. She must have something I could borrow. Well, maybe not borrow since I can't exactly give it back.

PS—She's probably at Sid's dorm, making out with him. Don't those two ever come up for air?

7:53 PM, EST

Pia! Claudia! Get me to a trauma center! I was just witness to something horrifying and I'm liable never to recover.

Samantha was out of pads, so she gave me her tampons instead. I didn't want to go there, but I also didn't trust my homemade adult diaper to get me through the night.

I've seen tampons before, but when I took one out of the box today, I saw it with new eyes.

Asking someone to fit that thing inside her you-know-what is downright nutty. Like asking someone to try and fit a Barbie doll up their nose. Actually, Lola does that all the time. See? Nutty.

Not knowing how to proceed, I consulted the instruction booklet that comes inside the box. I combed its pages, looking for a helpful hint. Something along the lines of, "Contrary to popular belief, actual insertion is unnecessary. Pretending to do so works just as well." But I couldn't find it. Not even in the fine print.

I'd even have settled for, "Close your eyes and make a wish. Tampon will self-insert." But all I found was, "Use a mirror to help guide you."

Whoever wrote that gobbledygook obviously does not have a vagina. Because if they did, there would have been a warning attached:

Beware: No matter what you've heard in health ed,

the vagina is not beautiful. Supermodels are beautiful. The vagina is pink and wrinkly. For those of you who attended Berkeley Middle School last year, the face of Mervis the librarian comes to mind.

Even that would not have prepared me for the shock I felt at what I saw. It looked like it didn't belong there. I'm just grateful that the mirror didn't break. The last thing I need is more bad luck. Or to have ruined something else that belongs to Samantha.

It took five tries and lots of deep breathing, but I eventually did get the tampon in. Without the help of the mirror, thank you very much. I will say that wearing it isn't nearly as bad as I thought it would be. I'm not even walking funny.

Promise me one thing. Do not make the same mistake I did. When you guys get your period, stay far away from the mirror. Trust me. The last sight you'll want to see is Mervis the librarian between your legs.

10:09 PM, EST

Me and Mervis are hitting the road. I kid you not, my time in this crazy household is over. If I needed a trauma counselor before, now I need a round-the-clock team of specialists.

Horse Ass just congratulated me on getting my period. Yes, you heard correctly, Horse Ass Bennett, with his

Grecian Formula hair and armpit-level-belted jeans came into my room, sat on my bed, punched me on the arm, and said, "Dudette, I hear you became a woman today."

Yuck. I need to wash my brain out with soap. If I had known my mom would go blabbing about it to every Tom, Dick, and Harry—not to mention Horace—I never would have shared such private information. Who can you trust these days?

And while we're on the subject, what on earth is a "dudette"? A dude with a bleeding Mervis?

Now that I'm an adult, it's time to take matters in my own hands. Going forward, if Horse Ass wants to talk to me, he'll have to bring me a letter of intent. Or at least a Pop-Tart.

Of course, if there were a way out of adulthood, I'd gladly take that route. It's done nothing for me but get me into trouble. If it weren't for my nasty period, I'd still be on the soccer team, we might not have lost the game, and the Fiona and Haileys would have no reason not to want my friendship.

Comments:

Logged in at 10:35 PM, EST

PiaBallerina: RAISIN!!!!!! I can't believe you got your period. And used a tampon on the first day. You deserve a medal of honor. I'm so glad you warned us about the mirror. I'm staying far away.

Logged in at 10:42 PM, EST

<u>kweenclaudia</u>: rae-rae, you're so full of surprises. i definitely thought i'd be the first. congratulations! but i do think you might be exaggerating how bad it looks down there. i've already checked mine out in the mirror. last year, after watching a tv special on human sexuality, and really, i don't see the big whoop. i mean, think about what boys have down there.

Friday, October 15

7:07 AM, EST

Kat Women,

Thanks, ladies. Claud, I'd rather not think about what boys have down there. If I wanted to go to the dark side, I'd have plenty of material to draw from much closer to home:

1. The fact that when the Fiona and Haileys see me today, they're going to clobber me.
2. The fact that when Jeremy sees me today, he's going to want to know when we can hang out with Fiona.
3. The fact that that date with Esther the cafeteria lady is starting to look good.

12:43 PM, EST

On the way up the school steps I saw Fiona, Hailey, and Madison. They were leaning against the railing—

laughing and whispering about something. Something really funny and secret, I'm guessing.

I felt like I should say something to make up for the big loss yesterday.

"Hey, guys," I said. They barely stopped to notice me.

"I just wanted to say that I'm really sorry about what happened at the game yesterday. I guess I didn't see the ball coming until it was too—"

I saw Fiona's mouth drop wide open, so I paused. She started pointing and making squealing noises. At first I thought she was doing this to me. Then I saw that she was looking over my shoulder. I heard the sound of footsteps behind me and turned around to see who it was.

It was Bliss, and she was dressed in an outfit almost identical to sassy student.

"You look amazing!" Fiona said to her.

"Where did you get that?" Madison asked.

"Can I borrow it sometime?" Hailey wanted to know.

It was my outfit! Bliss was dressed in my outfit! Those compliments belonged to me too!

"Bliss, it's so weird! I bought almost exactly the same outfit, but my mother—"

Suddenly, finishing that sentence no longer seemed like the greatest idea. What was I thinking? That broadcasting how my mother still treats me like a baby was somehow going to impress them?

"My mother accidentally threw it in the garbage," I said, slipping away as quickly as I could. Not that I needed to. For all they cared, I could have just continued standing there. Either way, they were bound to continue ignoring me.

I think it's time for me to give up. If they can't see by now that I'm just like them—that I think teachers with pubic hair coming out of their ears are funny too, and that I also like red leather bags with pink initials, and that I can pick out a fashionable outfit like sassy student as well as the next guy—then I don't know when they will.

12:45 PM, EST

On the bright side, Esther the cafeteria lady has warmed to me since yesterday. I think it's because I told her how much my mom loved the tuna casserole recipe.

"She's going to make it for us every Thursday night for dinner," I said to her as I reached for a hard-boiled egg.

A little white lie never hurt anyone, right?

"So zees ees vy you no eat my tuna casserole today?"

"Oh no, I'll have some," I said as I motioned for her to serve it to me. "I could never have enough of your tuna casserole," I told her. This white lie will actually hurt someone.

Me.

Because now I have to let her put that horrific mess on my plate every time it's on the menu.

Oh, well. It's the least I can do for a new pal. Though I'm not exactly sure where we stand. She still hasn't asked me out on that date. Maybe I'm supposed to ask her?

7:57 PM, EST

I had to have dinner at Jeremy's house again because my mom and what's-his-name had a business "engagement."

I was kind of dreading it all day because I was sure Jeremy would be angry with me. But when we met up by the steps after school, he was just as friendly as always.

"You're not mad at me for quitting the team?" I asked as we walked down the footpath that leads to the school parking lot.

"Why would I be?" he answered, picking up a twig and tossing it toward the school lawn.

"Cuz I promised that once I was friends with Fiona, I'd help you get together with her."

"Well, I don't think your being on the soccer team was helping any. I was at the Merion game. You were kind of a spaz. . . ."

I'd forgotten how harsh Jeremy could be at times.

"Maybe so. But please don't use that word. We in the spaz community prefer the term *athletically challenged*."

"Oh, okay, then. I won't."

I'll find away to make it up to him, though. I know I will. I haven't given up entirely. One day Fiona will see me for who I really am, and then the three of us can hang out together. Could be tomorrow . . . could be twenty years from now when we're all married with children of our own.

Saturday, October 16

7:03 PM, EST
Kittens,

Still have my period. Still have to face Those Who Refuse to Be My Friend on Monday.

Sunday, October 17

7:06 AM, EST
Kitty Cats,

I'd rather have a root canal on my butt than go to school tomorrow.

Scratch that last comment. It was immature and

unladylike. Now that I'm a woman, I should speak like a woman. What's more, it made no sense. . . .

I'd rather have a root canal on my *tooth* than go to school tomorrow.

7:08 AM, EST

Root canal on my tooth? Not as funny as root canal on my butt.

I think growing up means choosing between funny and ladylike. . . .

When did it all get so complicated?

PS—Where are you guys?

Comments:

Logged in at 8:51 PM, EST

<u>PiaBallerina</u>: Sorry, Rae. We were on the seventh-grade camping retreat.

Logged in at 8:59 PM, EST

<u>kweenclaudia</u>: i know things aren't going so great for you now, but think of it this way. at least you didn't have to spend the weekend sleeping on the ground, eating barbecue tofu burgers and peeing in the woods.

Logged in at 9:03 PM, EST

<u>PiaBallerina</u>: She's got a point.

Monday, October 18

7:08 AM, EST

Dear Kitties,

I wonder how Gordo dealt with not having friends. I mean I'm sure he had many friends on the earth. But he probably didn't have any in space.

7:10 AM, EST

I bet he has lots of friends in heaven, though.

5:06 PM, EST

Not to be disrespectful to Gordo's memory or anything, but I have more exciting news about CJ!

I guess I was kind of staring at him at dismissal today. I wasn't even aware of it until Sparkles found me at the bottom of the school entranceway staircase.

"New Girl, watch this," he said as he threw a piece of cardboard on the floor and lowered himself onto it. "I'm learning how to break dance. Whaddya think?" he asked as he spun around on his back with his knees folded up against his chest.

I guess I didn't answer him right away because he got to his feet and waved his hands in my face.

"Earth to New Girl," he said. Then he followed my gaze, which was fixed on CJ.

"Mmm-hmmm. I hear that loud and clear. He's a hottie. And his dads are really nice too."

"Dads? Whaddya mean?"

"See those two men with him?"

"Yeah, so?" I still wasn't getting it.

"New Girl. Wake up and smell the disco ball. CJ has two dads!"

"Ohhh. Now I get it," I said.

"Makes him even cuter, doesn't it?" Sparkles said as he folded up his cardboard. "Gotta go home and practice. Toodles!"

Sparkles was right. CJ's dads do make him cuter somehow—different. . . .

Maybe that's it. Maybe the reason he's so quiet is that he feels *different*. And maybe whatever's in the bag makes him feel different too. Maybe that's why he hides it.

I wish he didn't feel like he had to hide. It would make my job of figuring out the mystery of CJ so much easier.

PS—I hope I didn't offend Gordo by changing the subject, but I think he's the kind of monkey ghost who understands.

Comments:

Logged in at 8:06 PM, EST

<u>PiaBallerina</u>: CJ sounds so cute. And I get the feeling he's sweet too. Definitely sweeter than, say, your cous—I mean, sweeter than most boys.

Logged in at 8:11 PM, EST

<u>kweenclaudia</u>: and cuter than the delivery boy too. this morning he had a big whitehead on his nose. i couldn't even concentrate on what he was saying. all I could do was wonder why he hadn't popped it yet.

Tuesday, October 19

7:03 AM, EST

Hello Kitties,

I can't stop wondering about CJ. He's just not like any other boy I know:

1. He's quiet.
2. He's a math genius.
3. He smells like cinnamon.
4. He has two dads.
5. He's extremely good-looking—possibly gorgeous.
6. Yet he doesn't use his good looks to have his way with the ladies.
7. In fact, I've never even seen him speak to a lady.
8. Or a girl.
9. Or even Fiona (who's a girl, of course, but kind of in her own category because she's a sex goddess).
10. He's got that mysterious rolled-up shopping bag.

Maybe the key to the mystery of CJ is in the rolled-up shopping bag.

Maybe he's got a small friend in there. And the

friend, who smells like cinnamon, is the only person he actually converses with.

I must find out what's in the bag.

Because let's face it. It's definitely *not* a small friend.

4:57 PM, EST

Today they announced class elections. Fiona's running for president. And so is Jeremy's friend Roger Morris (of overgrown-seventh-grader fame). And some other girl I don't know. And then that alt guy who was eating lunch with CJ the other day. The one with green hair. But he's running on the Anarchy ticket, so I don't think we're allowed to vote for him.

I don't know why anyone's bothering to run against Fiona. It's not like they actually stand a chance at winning.

Wednesday, October 21

12:23 PM, EST

Dear Kitties,

Attention, Kmart shoppers . . . Stop the presses . . . Alert the masses . . . Hear ye, hear ye . . . I did it! . . . I dropped a snotty tissue in CJ's shopping bag and now we're in love!

12:31 PM, EST

GOOD GOD! I had to pee really badly, so I ran to the bathroom and didn't log off correctly.

Imagine if someone had found this!

Imagine if CJ had found this!

My life would be over!

7:36 PM, EST

Did you hear what I said before? CJ and I are in love.

7:55 PM, EST

L-O-V-E.

8:17 PM, EST

Anyone interested in the details?

8:19 PM, EST

Anyone at all?

8:21 PM, EST

Okay, okay, jeez.

If you're so insistent on knowing every little detail . . .

We'd really hoped to carry out our love affair away from the spotlight, but I see now that that's probably impossible.

Here goes. It's in the form of a poem, if that's okay.

What can I tell you? He brings out the poetry in me.

JUDY GOLDSCHMIDT

"The Snotty Tissue"
By
Raisin Rodriguez

Wait . . . Before I forget . . .

So we're all on the same page . . . Technically speaking, when I say we're in love, I actually mean *I'm* in love. But let's keep in mind . . . *I* is one half of *we*, so I . . . we . . . are halfway there. . . .

Now that we're clear . . .

"The Snotty Tissue"
By
Raisin Rodriguez

Roses are red,
Violets are blue,
I-accidentally-on-purpose-dropped-my-snotty-tissue-into-your-bag-since-I-knew-you-wouldn't-want-to-touch-it-and-when-I-dug-in-I-found-a-violin-which-is-the-cutest-thing-I've-ever-seen-in-my-life,
And now, CJ Mullen,
I love you.

CAN YOU EVEN?
A violin! He keeps it in its case! Which he lugs

around in a shopping bag, I think maybe because he's embarrassed. Because it's so different.

How cute is that?

So cute. That's how cute. Now I can say with full certainty that he is one hundred percent, without a doubt, grade-A gorgeous. (Like I said, for me, it's about the whole package.)

And what about me? How smart am I? The snotty tissue was a brilliant move. Even more brilliant than the pencil, which turned out to be kind of stupid. My one regret is not thinking of it sooner.

Now if only he had said, "Oh, Raisin, you've discovered my secret. I knew you'd understand. Let's forget about seventh grade and Fiona and Hailey. Let's give up our dreams of music and red leather bags with pink monograms and run away together," instead of, "I know how you feel. The pollen count is off the charts today," we might be getting somewhere.

I shouldn't complain. It's definitely a start. At least he knows how I feel.

9:48 PM, EST

He has no idea how I feel. He thinks I suffer from allergies. What I really suffer from is lovesickness.

9:51 PM, EST

Unless he's falling in love with me too. In that case I suffer from lovewellness.

Comments:
Logged in at 10:16 PM, EST

<u>PiaBallerina</u>: Ooh. He's a musician. How sexy.

PS—Maybe you shouldn't write to us from the school computer anymore? It'd be awful if you got caught. Everyone would know your secrets. And your personal stuff too. And you've got *lots* of personal stuff.

Logged in at 10:21 PM, EST

<u>kweenclaudia</u>: be careful, rae-rae. don't do anything hasty like drop out of school and follow him on tour. being a groupie never works out for the girl.

Thursday, October 21

4:53 PM, EST

Hello Kitties,

I'm really on a roll now.

First, CJ and I fall in love.

Then today, Fiona and I bonded like wild women!

. . . It didn't happen at all the way I imagined it would. She didn't ask me how I managed to discover what's in CJ's bag. She wasn't curious about my inspiration for the brilliantly hilarious nickname *Furguson*. Not once did she bring up Madonna. Or (and this one surprised me) ask me what Esther the cafeteria lady's *really* like. Plus the whole episode took place in the fourth-floor bathroom. I had pictured it happening in a dewy meadow or the shoe salon at Neiman Marcus. There I was, minding my own business, wiping a little leftover egg white off my cheek from this morning's DIY facial mask, when Fiona approached me. She was in a panic. Her eyes were spiraling in opposite directions and she looked ready to lift off into orbit.

"Raisin!" she said in a hushed tone. I wondered if she was whispering because she was embarrassed to be talking to me.

"Yeah?" I whispered back.

I don't think she heard me because she said it again.

"Raisin!"

"Yeah?" I answered, a little louder this time.

"I need to ask you a favor," she said.

I couldn't believe Fiona Small was actually coming to me for help.

"You wouldn't happen to have a pad, would you? I've asked everyone else, and no one's got any."

"Do you want a tampon?" I ventured.

The question seemed to frighten her. Maybe she's seen her Mervis too. I could have kicked myself for not anticipating her needs.

"I've never used one before. Maybe I should go to the nurse's office and get a pad instead."

"No," I warned her. "Whatever you do, do *not* go to the nurse's office. There are *boys* there just waiting around to see which girls have their periods so they can blab about it to the whole school." I'm not sure if that's true or not. But it's a good theory and it made me sound really knowledgeable.

"Have *you* ever used a tampon?" she asked. Her tone was drowning in skepticism. Like she was asking me if I ever operated heavy artillery or partied gangsta style. I guess she didn't see me as the tampon-using type.

"Many times," I answered, as if tampons were no big deal.

Fiona took a moment to pick her jaw up off the floor and regroup.

"Really? I mean, no offense, Raisin, but you are kind of a spaz."

I won't pretend that last comment didn't hurt. But I had to keep my eye on the prize. If I played my cards right, then maybe she'd finally allow me into her circle.

"Well, the spaz community prefers the term *athletically challenged,* but your point is well taken. If I can do it, so can a trained seal," I answered as I handed her the tampon. She held it in her hand for a while, just inspecting it.

"I can't," she said, her voice cracking as she looked both ways to make sure no one was around. Her eyes welled up with tears. "I'm scared."

Whoa, I thought. Fiona Small just admitted to me that she was scared. I was so surprised. I never knew anything could faze her.

"It's okay, Fiona, I was scared too. But it's not as bad as it looks. You kind of just have to go for it."

"I guess. I just wish my mother had gotten me pads like I asked her. Then I wouldn't have to deal with it," she said. Now Fiona sounded angry.

"Why didn't she?" I asked.

She hesitated for minute. "Come here," she said, and pulled me into the stall. "You have to promise not to tell anyone I was crying, okay?"

"I promise," I said.

"She forgot," Fiona started. "She's been pretty scattered lately. She and my dad are getting a divorce." Her voice cracked again when she told me this.

It's weird. I never thought of Fiona as someone who could be hurt by anything.

"I know how that is," I told her. "My parents got divorced two years ago, and my mom just remarried. Nothing's been the same since. I had to move away from my friends, I hardly see my mom anymore, and I have a new stepdad who calls me "dudette" and thinks it's okay to ask me about boys and a stepsister whose poodle is a drag queen."

"And do your friends understand what you're going through? Cuz I love my friends, but sometimes I don't feel like they understand at all."

For once I felt like the lucky one. I never feel like you guys don't understand. She's really got it rough.

Not too rough, though. She's still got a following of adoring admirers. Myself included.

"My friends are very understanding. . . . But they're all the way in Berkeley," I said. Then I figured I should leave her alone so she could do her thing. "I guess divorce just sucks no matter who you are. Anyway, good luck," I said. But as I reached for the door handle, Fiona took me by the shoulder and stopped me.

"Hey, Raisin," she started.

"Do you want me to wait outside for you?" I asked.

"Nah. I just wanted to say that I'm running for class president . . . but you probably know that already. . . . And that I could use an extra person on my campaign committee . . ."

"Oh, I get it. So I can be there for you if you want to talk about the divorce. Like if you need support or something."

"Actually, I was thinking you could help with the posters."

Friday, October 22

8:01 PM, EST

Dear Felines,

The first campaign meeting was great. It was like I was one of the girls. No one mentioned the awkward soccer apology. Or the awkward birthday moment. Hailey didn't mention the awkward algebra study session, either. It must be hard for her to keep track of all the awkward moments she's not supposed to mention.

As Fiona got organized, Hailey, Madison, and Bliss asked me questions about what it's like to grow up in Berkeley. Then Bliss dropped the clunker:

"Is Jeremy your boyfriend?" she asked.

"No, Jeremy's just a friend," I said as slowly, loudly, and clearly as I could.

"That's too bad. He's kinda cute," Madison added.

It's strange, I never really thought of him that way. I did check on Fiona to see if I could detect a flicker of agreement in her eyes. That would make my job of getting them together so much easier. There was a bit of a twinkle. I wasn't sure if it was in response to

Jeremy or her own reflection. She'd been admiring herself in the classroom window.

I asked them some questions too. This is what I found out:

1. None of them have boyfriends right now except for Hailey, who's still kind of going out with Mike Leary.
2. None of them have ever noticed how gorgeous CJ is.
3. None of them have ever heard him speak to anyone but a teacher.

Which means I'm the only kid he's ever spoken to. Makes me feel pretty special.

Once the meeting commenced, we figured out a perfect platform for Fiona: A Vote for Fiona Is a Vote for a More Beautiful School. . . .

Kinda says it all.

PS—Turns out the posters are going to be a little more difficult to make than I thought. Oak tag, Magic Markers, and a little Rae love isn't going to cut it. They were talking clip art, Photoshop, and laser printers. I mean, who do they think I am, some kind of computer genius?

Comments:

Logged in at 8:32 PM, EST

kweenclaudia: rae, you don't have to be a computer genius to figure out how to use clip art. it's just like soccer. anyone can do it. oops! bad example! sorry!

Logged in at 8:42 PM, EST

<u>PiaBallerina</u>: Claud's right. It's easy. Pretty much anyone can explain it you.

9:47 PM, EST

Great! I'm all ears!

Comments:

Logged in at 10:14 PM, EST

<u>kweenclaudia</u>: jeremy'll do it.

Logged in at 10:17 PM, EST

<u>PiaBallerina</u>: What she said.

Monday, October 25

7:06 AM, EST

My Furry Friends,

I'm not sure Jeremy can do it. I mean, he can't be good at everything, can he?

Can't wait to sit at Fiona's table during lunch. I'm wearing my dad's red boots in honor of the occasion. Gotta go!

12:46 PM, EST

Ever since the campaign meeting, I'd been picturing what it would be like to finally eat lunch at Fiona's table. Down to the very last details. The snappy exchange of witty remarks . . . the secrets traded . . . the knowing glances . . . the honor of being the only out-sider invited to sit with them (i.e., the distinct absence of Jeremy Craine).

Guess which detail was off . . .

I was standing in line, waiting for my hard-boiled egg, when he got behind me and threw me off my guard. You'd think I'd have caught on to his ways by now, but with all I've had on my mind lately, some-thing had to give.

Still, I needed his help with the posters, so it wasn't all bad news.

"Hey, Jer, guess what? I'm on Fiona's campaign committee. The only thing is she wants me to make posters, and I don't really know how. Think you can help me out?" I asked.

"I'm not sure. Roger asked me to be his campaign manager, so I don't think he'd be too cool with that," he answered, reaching for his cottage cheese and peaches.

Sometimes Jeremy can be so by the rules.

"Look, I'm sure this isn't the first time he's run for seventh-grade president, and it probably won't be the last. . . ."

"I don't know, Rae . . ." He was just playing hard-ball with me, and I knew exactly what he was after.

"I promise to invite you to hang out with me and Fiona as we start getting closer."

"You promised me the same thing last time," he said.

"Exactly. And what happened last time? I screwed up. But if you help out with the posters, then there's very little chance of that."

"Well, I am really good at that stuff, so I guess it could only help," he said. So, he can make posters. One thing I have to say about him—he's quite multi-talented.

By this time we were already standing by Fiona's table. She invited me to sit down. But instead of leaving to play sweat hockey with his friends, Jeremy just hovered over the table. He turns into such a dodo-head when it comes to her. It's like all the leering and drooling eats into any leftover brainpower he might have.

My strategy was to continue as if he wasn't there and hope that he'd eventually go away, leaving me to bask in my moment.

"Hey, Fiona, what's up?" I asked.

Then I noticed her head was under the table and her hands were tugging at the loops on my boots.

"Where'd you get these?" she asked.

"In Berkeley. Actually, my dad got—"

"What store?" she asked, before I could finish my sentence.

"Bloomingdale's," I answered. "I'd had my eye on them since—" This time I cut myself off.

"Do you think they sell them at the Bloomingdale's here?"

"Well, Philly buyers tend to have more conservative tastes than California buyers as a rule. But you never know what they might throw in the mix just to keep consumers interested."

That little nugget did not come from me. Or anyone sitting at the table. Or even a girl. It came from Jeremy. He'd been so quiet and gawky, I'd almost forgotten he was standing there. Then when he finally came back to life, he sounded like an editor from *Teen Vogue*. I can't really say I understood his game plan.

"Jeremy, why don't you sit down and tell us how you know so much about shoes?" Fiona said with a toss of her blond locks.

"My mom's a buyer for Neiman Marcus," he said, wasting no time in taking Fiona up on her offer. Then he pulled a chair up *between* me and Fiona. I did not work so hard at getting her to like me just to have Jeremy sit between us. But once Fiona heard about Jeremy's mother, she fastened on him. I couldn't tear them away from each other.

I brought up many interesting topics ranging from blue Oreos (disgusting or delightful?) to trance versus trip-hop, but they just continued to chatter away like the best of girlfriends. All I can say is that Jeremy better not come crying to me if Fiona never sees him as boyfriend material.

I turned to Madison, who was saying something to Hailey and Bliss about girls' basketball tryouts. All around me, I was being shut out by people's conversations.

So there I was, kind of just stuck, eating my hard-boiled egg. I managed to separate the yolk from the white part in one piece, so I wouldn't say lunch was a total loss.

If I can't get self-worth from my talent with people, I can always get it from my talent with eggs.

4:36 PM, EST

I called Jeremy after school to see when he could help me with the posters. He said tomorrow would work. Then he asked me if I thought Fiona might like him.

On the one hand, maybe she does. But on the other hand, she probably does not.

I told him to wait before he does anything. That even if she does like him, he might as well not risk asking her out until I find out for sure. I just don't want to see his little freckled heart broken.

8:36 PM, EST

The good news: Fiona asked me to go shopping with her tomorrow. She needs an outfit for election day.

Yippee! I'm still popular!

The weird news: she asked me for Jeremy's number too.

Could he be right? Could she actually like him?

8:57 PM, EST

I just called Jeremy to tell him I'd have to skip the poster-making. And guess what?

Fiona invited him to go shopping too!

She said she wanted a male opinion since boys make up 49 percent of the vote. Who else did she invite? Esther the cafeteria lady? I mean, we probably shouldn't forget how much of the vote is represented by the food service industry.

It's not fair! It's all because of that conversation they had at lunch today. My invitation just doesn't seem as special now. It almost seems like I only got it so that Fiona could get Jeremy's number from me.

Interesting how suddenly Jeremy doesn't care so much about making Roger angry . . . or mind helping me with my posters. . . .

He said he'd do them after shopping.

I hope there's enough time.

Tuesday, October 26

8:37 PM, EST

Hello, my Kittens,

Just got back from shopping. As much as I didn't want Jeremy to come along, I have to say, we really needed him there. He definitely inherited his mother's gene for shopping.

We all made our own suggestions for outfits. I picked out a shirt and tie. Very punk rock but also very presidential at the same time.

Madison picked out something Chanel-y. A short plaid jacket with a gold chain belt, blue jeans, and pumps.

Bliss wanted her to wear a skirt suit. Simple, but very official looking.

But Jeremy's outfit was by far the best.

"Your platform is For a More Beautiful School, right? Well, then you should wear something *beautiful.*" He made a good point. He made it loudly, but it was definitely good.

I thought, *Oh no, here comes the prom dress and the tiara.* But what he brought out *was* genuinely beautiful. A pastel-patterned chiffon blouse with bell sleeves that ties in a bow in the back, and black wool pants. And when Fiona came out of the dressing room, she looked absolutely beautiful. Not froufrou beautiful either. Smart beautiful.

"See, I knew I needed you along," Fiona said.

Jeremy's mom picked us up from the mall. In the car I asked him how he knew which outfit to pick out.

"I asked the saleslady," he said.

Now, why couldn't I have thought of that?

It's all right. At least I still have my posters to impress Fiona with. Well, Jeremy's posters, actually. . . . The more I get to know that guy, the better I like him.

And he made me look good too. He told the girls that I have a good sense of humor. And the story of how I thought of taking funny pictures with his camera phone and sending them to the *Troubadour*. And that I'm cool because I'm the first girl to ever sit alone at his friends' table.

So even though I didn't come up with the winning outfit and even though I wanted to be the only one invited along, it wasn't so bad having Jeremy there.

Plus, he's so psyched about hanging out with Fiona that he told me not to even worry about the posters. He'll take care of the whole thing and bring them in for me tomorrow.

Comments:

Logged in at 9:46 PM, EST

<u>PiaBallerina</u>: See how quickly things turn around?

Logged in at 9:53 PM, EST

<u>kweenclaudia</u>: p's right. this is kind of difficult for me to say . . . but . . . i'm really proud of you!

Wednesday, October 27

12:07 PM, EST

Kitty Claudia and Kitty Pia,

Guess what? Bliss invited me to her Halloween party!

I'm living my dream life of wild popularity! Yippee!

I've already decided that I'm going as a gypsy. I'll wear lots of scarves and dangling jewelry, and I'll take that heinous pink gauze skirt out of hiding and finally put it to good use. Then to top it off, I'm going to carry around a Magic 8 Ball and tell people's fortunes. Maybe find out some juicy little tidbits in the process!

In a related story, Fiona was a little mad at me today. She thought I'd have the posters ready by this morning. So did I, actually. Jeremy was supposed to have printed them out at his house. But his printer broke. So he e-mailed the files to me so I could print them out at school.

Oh, well. Here they come.

Bye for now!

From: RaisinRodriguez@bennetco.com
Sent: Wednesday, October 28, 2:29 PM
To: kweenclaudia@homelink.net, PiaBallerina@brkly.rr.com
Subject: Change of Plans

My new blog address is
www.NoneofYourBeesWax.blogspace.com.
www.TwoScoopsofRaisin.com has been permanently
and irrevocably deleted.

Will explain later. Gotta go.

Thursday, October 28

4:31 PM, EST

Friends and Kittens,

Thank you for coming to www.NoneofYourBeesWax.blogspace.com. Though I feel it only fair to warn you that the girl who writes it may very well be the biggest idiot in the whole wide world. Not to mention the biggest nincompoop and also the biggest butthead. Dingbat, ding-dong, ding-a-ling, dope, lamebrain, numskull, knucklehead, moron, half-wit, imbecile, and, my personal favorite, chowderhead.

So you might want to stay very far away from her in case it's contagious.

I suppose I should tell you what happened, but you

have to promise not to yell at me. Or say, "I told you so," even though you did. Or judge me in any way.

Promise?

Okay, here goes:

After I typed up my last entry, I made printouts of the poster files Jeremy had sent me. Then I went to gym.

This month we're doing a karate unit. As a member of the athletically challenged community, I like it because I can actually participate. There are no complicated rules to follow, no balls to drop, and no teammates to disappoint, so there's less opportunity for anyone to get angry with me. (Well, except this one girl who I accidentally kicked in the nose last time.)

Today we were working on karate chops. It was almost my turn to go when through the tiny window I saw a hand waving at me. It was covered in freckles, so I knew it had to belong to Jeremy. I was going to just ignore him until after my turn, but the waving got so frantic, it seemed like something important was up.

I got permission to leave the gym and met Jeremy outside.

"Didn't you see me?" Jeremy started. He was huffing and puffing, which concerned me. If a little hand waving was enough to wear him out like that, I thought that maybe he should consider a strength-training program.

"I've been trying to get your attention for like ten minutes," he continued, taking a deep breath. "I have something really important to ask you," he started.

Something important? I wondered. *What could that be?*

"It's kind of personal, though," he continued.

My mind went back to the time he saw me in the nurse's office after I got my period. I prayed it had nothing to do with that.

"How personal?" I asked.

"Do you keep a blog by any chance?" he responded.

I had to have misheard him.

"I'm sorry, what'd you say?" I asked.

"I said, do you keep a blog by any chance. . . ."

This time I knew I heard him correctly. My heart started to race. He might as well have asked me if I accidentally pulled my pants down in front of the entire school.

"What are you saying, Jeremy?" I asked in a hushed tone. "What do you know?"

"Roger Morris told me he saw a page of something called *Two Scoops of Raisin* up on one of computers, and when he read it, it seemed like it could be yours. . . ."

For a second the world turned black. When the colors came back, so did my memory. I realized I must have done it again—I must have forgotten to log out of my blog before printing out Fiona's campaign posters.

And worse, that the entry on the screen was probably the one about Jeremy not being able to print the posters out in time for school today. That's probably what caught Roger's eye in the first place—his opponent's name.

How stupid could I be?

Actually, that's a stupid question. Judging from today's events . . . EXTREMELY, SUPREMELY, HIDEOUSLY, ONE BILLIONLY, FORFEITS-THE-RIGHT—TO-EVER-CALL-ANYONE-ELSE (TODDLERS AND OVERGROWN POODLES INCLUDED)-STUPID-FOR-THE-REST-OF-HER-LIFE-SO-HELP-HER-GOD *STUPID*. THAT'S HOW STUPID.

My mind raced. I felt dizzy and my breathing got choppy. What if Roger left my blog on the screen? What if he shared the address with other people? What if the Fiona and Haileys read it? What if . . .

"Jeremy, did you read the blog?"

"No, Raisin. Of course not. That would be like reading someone's diary. I could never do a thing like that."

Thank heavens, I thought. *I will never say, write, feel, or think anything bad about Jeremy ever again.*

"That's really nice of you. I don't know how to thank you."

"Don't worry about it, Raisin. That's what friends are for."

He was right. And I had to be a good friend back. So

I told him that if Roger read the part of the blog I think he read, he probably knows that Jeremy was helping out with Fiona's posters. It seemed only fair.

"Good to know," he said rather calmly.

"What are you going to do?" I asked.

"I'll tell him it's cuz I'm so into her. He'll understand."

"Aren't you afraid he'll be mad at you?" I asked.

"Nah. As long as I stay on as his campaign manager and promise to still vote for him, he'll understand."

I must have looked confused because he added, "It's a guy thing."

"I'm so sorry that I got you in trouble, Jeremy," I said.

"It's all good. I got to meet Fiona out of it," he said, kind of skipping toward the stairs.

I raced back to the gym and told the teacher I needed to see the nurse as soon as possible. He told me to go ahead. That's the one good thing about hitting puberty. You can always say you need to "see the nurse." Especially to men. They never question you on it because they don't really like to think about it for too long.

I made it up to the computer room in record time. But I was so frazzled that when the blog site asked me for my password, I blanked. I use that password whenever I log on. But for the life of me, I couldn't remember it this time. Of all times! And I only had a few minutes to spare before my next class!

In order for me to get the password, I had to fill out a form that sends it to my e-mail, check my e-mail, and wait until the password was sent. Then I had to log on to my blog, and fill out the form that deletes it, and double-check to make sure it was deleted properly.

The password, by the way, was my old phone number in Berkeley.

I did it, but with only thirty seconds to make it to my next class. It's against the rules to come to class in sweats, and there was no time to stop in the bathroom, so I put my jeans on *over* my sweats. For the record, this is not a good look. But I was so relieved about destroying the evidence, I didn't care.

Hopefully, no one else had a chance to read it before I did.

Comments:

Logged in at 8:03 PM, EST

<u>PiaBallerina</u>: Jeez, Rae. That was so close. I guess you've gotta be extra careful from now on.

Logged in at 8:10 PM, EST

<u>kweenclaudia</u>: or you could just take it to the next level . . . go wide with it . . . let everyone know how you really feel . . . tell it like it is . . . the truth will set you free . . .

11:47 PM, EST

Thanks, Claud. But I'm probably not ready to go wide just yet. I spent most of the last three hours with my head between my legs trying not to hyperventilate. I can't stop thinking about what could have happened between the time Roger saw what he saw and the time I deleted it. What if it's out? Everyone will find out what I thought about them: Hailey will find out I thought she was a bit dull between the ears. Roger will find out that I joke about him being left back. Jeremy's friends will find out that I think they're sweaty.

No one was spared. Not even that girl Kim Weingarten who picks at her old mosquito bites until they bleed. What did she ever do to me?

And then there's all the embarrassing stuff about me. The way I got out of the soccer game. My love for CJ . . . My desperation to be accepted by the Fiona and Haileys. And what about Jeremy? If he had read the blog . . . I don't know what I would have done. . . .

So from now on, I'm going to stick with Pia's advice from before and only write to you guys from home.

Friday, October 29

12:01 PM, EST

Kitties,

Okay . . . so here I am, writing from school. Even

though we decided it wasn't such a smart thing to do. But something really funny happened and I just had to share. I think you guys will laugh about this one. Oh ha ha ha ha ha.

Remember how I listed all the parts of the blog that I wouldn't have wanted people to read? The parts that were so embarrassing, I couldn't have shown my face around school anymore? You know what I completely forgot to include on the list?

Mervis . . .

You know what reminded me?

Passing Mike Leary on the way into math class and hearing him say, "Hey, Mervis!" to me.

That really brought it back, loud and clear.

Actually, that was only the first of several reminders. Right after attendance during homeroom, a group of boys formed a huddle in the back of the room and chanted, "Go, Mervis, go, Mervis, it's your birthday, it's your birthday. . . ."

There was the eighth grader I don't even know who handed me his cell phone and said, "It's for you, Mervis. . . ."

And then there was Roger Morris, who threw a tampon at me in the hallway and yelled, "Watch out, Mervis!" I shouldn't really lump him in the same category as the others. If anything, he was being thoughtful. If he hadn't given me the heads-up, that thing could have poked me right in the eye.

Throughout the day there was much pointing, whispering, and glaring coming from the Fiona and Haileys.

I wonder how everyone found out. Could Roger have spread the word so quickly? Not that it matters. After I say goodbye to Jeremy, I'm digging a tunnel to Japan.

12:03 PM, EST

AAAAAAAAAAAAAAAHHHHHHHHHHHH!

12:04 PM, EST

No, No, No, No, No, No, No, No, No!

12:05 PM, EST

I AM GOING TO VOMIT. VOMIT! I WILL HAVE TO LEARN TO SAY VOMIT IN JAPANESE.

12:06 PM, EST

!!!!!!!!!!!!!!!!!!!!!

12:07 PM, EST

I suppose you could say there's a bright side to all this. Let's not forget that two days ago I was nobody. And today . . .

well . . .

. . . today, I'm Mervis.

12:08 PM, EST

But I think we'd all know what a sad, pathetic, heartbreaking lie that would be. The truth is that I used to be a nobody, and now I'm just a freakish nobody. I have done some deep yoga breaths and centered myself and now I have accepted the truth. *That's* why no one wants to be friends with me. Not because they haven't realized how great I am. But because they've known I'm a reject all along.

I'm just a freakish reject who does perverted embarrassing disgusting things like looking at her vagina in the mirror, naming it the way a normal person might name a pet, and then writing about it for her friends back home because no one else will bother with her.

I can't even leave school because I'm already in trouble for cutting class. I can't play sick because by now everyone knows me and my little playing-sick tricks. And for some strange reason, I can't even cry. The tears won't come.

Is there such a thing as being too upset to cry?

I'm going to go find Jeremy. I need to talk to him. I think it will make me feel better.

12:14 PM, EST

Turns out Roger didn't tell everyone about Mervis.

No, he just handed out printed copies of the blog and let everyone read about it for themselves!

I discovered this while braving the cafeteria to find Jeremy. First, a boy from earth science stopped to tell me he could cure my nippyitis if I let him examine me. I pretended not to hear him, gave my nips a secret check to make sure they weren't all over the place, and kept plowing through the crowd.

Then a girl from my soccer team apologized to me, saying that if she knew I was a mental patient she wouldn't have complained so bitterly about me to the coach. I also pretended not to hear her, but I made sure to put on a very sane face so she'd know I wasn't crazy.

But when Galenka said, "Eet eez true in America that doggies eat brassieres for deenner?" I cracked. I didn't have the strength to pretend anymore. Was there anyone left who hadn't read the blog?

"Galenka, how do *you* know about the dog? What, did your translator tell you about it or something?"

"I read about him myself, een blog."

"Where did you get the blog?" I asked.

"Roger Morris, he geeve it to me."

What a jerk! That gigantic mass of jiggly Jell-O must have given it to everyone!

I will say this, though, Galenka's English is getting a lot better.

By the time I made it to Jeremy's table, the tears that wouldn't come before were ready to pour out. But I had to hold on to them long enough to make it past his friends.

As soon as Jeremy and his boys saw me, they all went silent. I was prepared for someone to make a snide comment, but no one did. I took this as a promising sign. Like that maybe they'd go easy on me.

"Jeremy," I said in an almost-whisper. "Can I talk to you in private?"

He didn't say anything. I thought maybe he didn't hear me, so I repeated myself.

"Hey. Can we talk?"

This time he shot Roger a look. Roger nodded back.

"Why don't you ask someone who counts," Jeremy said, his face never redder.

Did I say he didn't count? If I did, I only meant he didn't count as a *new* friend. Because he's a friend of the family.

"I thought you weren't going to read it," I said.

"I didn't," he answered. "I didn't have to. Roger told me everything you said."

"Yup," Roger said. "It's right here, on September 22 . . . 'except for Jeremy, who doesn't count.'" Roger passed me a printout of the blog and showed it to me. "Right after you wrote about how the boys at this table sweat too much," he added. I looked around the table. They all looked pretty burned up about that one.

I felt horrible. Like the meanest, cruelest, most heartless person in the world. Especially after all the nice things Jeremy had done for me.

"Jeremy, I'm so sorry. But if you'd read my new blog, you'd have seen all the nice things I've written about you there."

"Yeah, of course you said nice things. I did everything I could to save your butt. Why wouldn't you say nice things?"

He had a point.

"But what about all the stuff I said about having fun at your house and about how great you were on the night we went shopping?" I asked.

"September 16 and October 26, respectively," Roger added. Boy, did I want to clock him. But like I've said, he's got a good foot and a half on me.

"Yeah, but you also acted like you were just putting up with me. Both times."

God, he knew that blog well. What did Roger do? Read the entire thing to him from cover to cover?

"Jeremy, I know you probably won't want to hear this right now. But I was wrong about you. I was wrong about everything I said. I guess I took you for granted because I already knew you and I wanted to see what else was out there. But that was a huge mistake. You're probably the nicest person I've ever met. And . . . I'm . . . really . . . really . . . sor—"

And then it happened. The dam broke. The floodgates opened. The tears came rushing out of me like a monsoon. I heard the boys' snickers. I saw their smirks through the blur. And there wasn't a thing I could do about it but run out of the cafeteria, praying that no one else would see me blubbering like a little baby.

But of course someone did.

"Hey, New Girl, wait up! You're like a celebrity or somethin'!"

But I couldn't wait up. Not even for Sparkles. I had to get to my place in the stairwell where I could be alone and sob my eyes out in peace.

7:53 PM, EST

This day keeps getting more and more strange. . . .

After my last entry, I fell asleep. I think I was exhausted from crying so much. When I woke up, I was struck with an epiphany.

The open plane ticket!

I'd totally forgotten about it!

I could use it to fly back to Berkeley!

It was the perfect solution!

I mean, it would kind of make me one of those problem-child-type kids, but I could live with that. It seemed like a small price to pay in exchange for salvaging my pride. And sure, my dad would be angry at first, but I know he'd forgive me as soon as he heard what had happened. Then I could live with him and see you guys every day, and I wouldn't even have to keep this stupid blog because, well, I'd be seeing you every day!

I started packing my bags immediately. At first I was only going to bring one small carry-on. It'd be easier to sneak out that way. But I couldn't fit my red boots in there. Or my laptop. Or all my new clothes from Giselle's. Or the purple velvet comforter on my bed. I never realized how much I loved that thing.

There was no way around it. I needed to take my big suitcase, which was all the way up on the top shelf of my closet. Even the biggest chair in my room wasn't tall enough to get me there, so I had to pile on a *Webster's* dictionary, a thesaurus, and my old pal, the earth science textbook. I climbed on top of the heap and grabbed the suitcase. But as I was pulling at the handle, the earth science book slipped, and I went crashing to the floor with a gigantic thud.

Before I could even get back on my feet, Samantha was standing over me.

"Raisin, what're you doing?" she asked, looking around the room. There were piles of clothes sitting on my bed. My comforter was folded up neatly and my toiletry bag was in plain sight. Between that and the gigantic suitcase that was lying on top of my chest, it wouldn't have taken a genius to figure out what was going on. And Samantha . . . well, she *is* a genius.

"Practicing fire safety. I'm timing myself to see how quickly I can get out of here with all of my belongings."

The look on her face said she wasn't buying it. Again, the genius thing . . .

"Here, let me help you," she said as she lifted the suitcase off from on top of me. "Raisy, I hope you know you can talk to me about anything that's bothering you. . . ."

"Okay. I'll do that," I said.

"I mean it. I know that you and I are different, but that doesn't mean I can't understand what you're going through."

What was I going through? What did she know about that she wasn't telling me? She was making me really nervous.

"Thanks, Sam. I'll keep it in mind."

"Because you know, sometimes middle school gossip travels . . ."

Oh no! I thought. Someone told her about the blog.

And that she and Sid were in it. After I *swore* not to tell . . .

It was all becoming clear to me. Samantha was there to rearrange my face. And just when I was starting to like her!

"Uh-huh," I said. I was trembling so hard, I had to crawl into bed and get under the covers to hide it.

"And today I heard this story about a seventh-grade girl who had a crush on a boy, and when she tried to talk to him, she threw up mushroom soup and it landed in his violin case. Do you know her?"

"Nuh-uh," I said, wondering whether she was bluffing. Whether she knew that girl was me and mixing up the details was her crafty little way of getting me to confess.

"Anyway, it just reminded me of how difficult middle school can be sometimes," she said, taking a seat at the edge of my bed. Which immediately made me think she was going to smother me with a pillow.

"And I realized, for the first time, that it must be doubly hard for you, being new and all," she said, putting her arm around me. "I think it'd be nice if we spent a little more time together. Maybe you wanna come to my room? You pick out a DVD to watch. I've got a ton of them."

Always full of surprises, that Samantha. I didn't even know she watched movies. I really wanted to take her up on her offer, but it seemed a bit risky. What if she just wanted to get me into her room because that's where she was hiding the murder weapon?

"Raisin?"

"I'm not sure. . . ."

"I'll make some popcorn."

"Popcorn?" I asked.

She nodded. Even if she was planning to rub me out, popcorn and a movie wasn't a bad way to go.

I decided to take her up on her offer.

I went to her room, and she went downstairs to make the popcorn. Whether she laced it with poison or not remains to be seen. But as of now (8:56 PM, EST), my vitals seem stable.

"Raisin, why are you sitting so far away from the TV?" she asked when she got back upstairs. I had moved one of her chairs over to the bathroom doorway. In case I needed to make a quick getaway to my room.

"Why don't you make yourself comfortable?" she asked, motioning for me to join her on the bed.

It gets even crazier.

"Raisin, you've done such a great job keeping Sid a secret, I want to tell you one more," she said. She had to be kidding me with that line. Either she was going to pull the trigger at that moment, or she really didn't know her secret was out.

"This may sound weird, but Countess is a boy. I just dress her like a girl."

I almost choked on an unpopped kernel.

"You're kidding. I never would have guessed. Are you positive?"

"Of course I am. Who knows? Maybe I was trying to make her into the little sister I never had. But that was before you came along," she said. And then she gave me a little squeeze.

And I gave her a little squeeze back. Because that's what sisters do.

10:37 PM, EST

Just got off the phone with Jeremy. I wanted him to know that even if he and I never spoke again, that shouldn't stop him from making a play for Fiona.

I referred him to the Friday, October 22, entry, where I detected "a twinkle" in Fiona's eyes at the mention of Jeremy's name. Needless to say, Roger had already read him that entry.

"So, ask her out," I said.

"I can't," he said.

"Why not?" I asked.

"Because she's probably read your blog too," he began. "And now she knows I have freckles." I felt for him. Not because of what he was saying, though that also made me feel for him. But because of how he sounded. When he said the word *freckles,* his voice went up three octaves. It sounded exactly like the noise Countess makes when someone accidentally steps on his tail.

"Jeremy, everyone knows about your freckles. They're right on your face."

"What about the fact that now she knows I did all those favors for you on the outside chance that it could bring me closer to her?" he added.

I'd forgotten about that.

"Right . . . Well . . . I'm sure you'll find someone else. . . . There are plenty of girls who'd be happy to go out with you."

Maybe that was lame, but what else could I say? He was right. Fiona could never respect someone who'd go to such lengths for her. She needed someone who could show her some backbone.

It was time to face facts. I had blown everything. Not just for me, but for Jeremy too. I could say I'm sorry a million times. But it wouldn't change a thing. I'm a horrible person and now I just have to live with it.

Comments:

Logged in at 11:37 PM, EST

PiaBallerina: Raisin, I feel so terrible about all of this. I wish I could be there for you. I know it seems impossible right now, but things will work out, I know it. Even with Jeremy. He just needs some time.

Logged in at 11:46 PM, EST

<u>kweenclaudia</u>: it's true, raisin. you can't see it now, but one day this will all be behind you and all you'll be left with is a really funny story to tell at parties!

Sunday, October 31

5:43 PM, EST

Kitty Cats,

Everyone's at Bliss's Halloween party having the time of their lives except for me.

The 8 Ball says: "You are *such* a loser."

Monday, November 1

7:00 AM, EST

Kitty Cats,

I don't know how I'm going to get through school today.

I tried playing sick, but as usual, my mother didn't fall for it. Even when I warmed the thermometer between my hands to make the temperature go up. She just felt my forehead and reminded me that there are so many children less fortunate than I who'd give anything for the opportunity to go to a nice school like mine. I'm sure those children have it rough, but I'm not buying the part about them wanting to go to my school so badly. They may be unfortunate, but they're not stupid.

I suppose I would have had to go anyway. I haven't given Fiona her posters yet.

I haven't had the guts to.

12:23 PM, EST

CJ hasn't said a word to me since the catastrophe started. Then again, he never talks to me unless I'm snooping around in his shopping bag. So it doesn't necessarily mean anything.

12:33 PM, EST

But it doesn't necessarily mean nothing either. He could have read the snotty tissue poem and be utterly disgusted by my outpouring of love.

12:43 PM, EST

Which brings up a good question: If he never talks to me, how will I ever know?

5:06 PM, EST

I think it's safe to say that Fiona, Hailey, Bliss, and Madison officially hate me.

I wanted to just drop by the campaign meeting room, hand the posters to Fiona, and leave. But when I got to the room, Hailey was the only person there.

"Can you give these to Fiona for me?" I asked her.

"I'm not sure what you mean by that. After all, I am a bit dull between the ears."

Okay, I thought, *maybe I should wait for Fiona in the hallway.*

But Madison and Bliss got there before her too.

"Hey, guys, would you mind just giving these to Fiona?" I asked as they passed me on the way inside the meeting room.

Bliss wouldn't even glance in my direction.

"You mean Fiona of the Fiona and Haileys?" Madison asked.

I guess they were insulted by my nickname for their group. I never even meant anything bad by that. I just used it because it was shorter than writing out their full names!

I had no choice but to wait for Fiona myself.

As soon as she laid eyes on me, she snatched the posters right out of my hands.

I tried to slip away before it came to blows.

"Not so fast, Raisin. Let's take a look at your little boyfriend's work." She unrolled the posters.

"He's not my boyf—" I protested.

"Nice," she said, cutting me off as usual. "These

better do the trick," she warned as she rolled the posters back up. "Because if I lose this election," she continued, tapping the edge of the rolled-up posters into her left palm, "you're in big trouble." Then she stormed into the meeting room.

The election! It never even occurred to me that my blog would affect the election.

All I know is that Fiona can*not* lose this election. I'll have to do everything in my power to make sure she wins.

5:15 PM, EST

But I don't have any power. Everyone hates me.

5:17 PM, EST

I must creatively visualize Fiona winning.

5:18 PM, EST

And repeat the mantra: "Fiona must win."

5:19 PM, EST

And light some sage.

5:20 PM, EST

Thank goodness Fiona is extraordinarily popular. I know this crunchy granola hoo-ha works for my dad, but if it were all I had to rely on, I'd be in big trouble.

Comments:

Logged in at 8:37 PM, EST

<u>PiaBallerina</u>: Rae-rae, I don't like Fiona. She seems kind of nasty. I think you're better off without her.

Logged in at 8:46 PM, EST

<u>kweenclaudia</u>: i'm with pi on this one. i might be the kween. but she's the queen of mean. you are so much better off without her.

Tuesday, November 2

7:07 AM, EST

Kittens,

Maybe I am better off without her. Which works out well, since she's obviously better off without me.

12:37 PM, EST

Kittens,

I'm resolved to stay strong and keep in mind that there are plenty of people worse off than me.

Think of Gordo. Gordo was a monkey, not a person, I know. But monkeys aren't *that* different from very furry people.

He *really* had it bad. He survived his trip around the earth. He made it all the way back to the ground. He was just about to complete his mission. But then his rocket landed in the ocean with him stuck inside the nose cone. And that was that.

Gordo.

Astronaut. Hero. Monkey.

His story makes my heart hurt.

Wednesday, November 3

5:07 pm, EST

Kitteny Kittens!

I'm not sure, but I might not be a loser anymore. . . .

I picked up my lunch from the cafeteria and brought it to my usual spot in the stairwell. (Esther almost didn't give it to me, by the way. She said that if I wanted to eat in her cafeteria again, I'd better replace the mushroom soup I took. "How'd you find out about that?" I asked her. "Vas een blog, of course," she answered.) There were already people sitting there, so I turned around to leave. Then I heard someone calling my name. It was that girl Kim Weingarten—the one with the mosquito bites.

"Raisin, I was hoping to find you here!" she said, following me up the stairs.

Someone was *hoping* to find me?

"I know from reading your blog that you come here sometimes. I think that thing is awesome."

She thought my blog was awesome? Did I understand correctly? I'd been staring at the bread crumb
stuck to her black lipstick, so I thought maybe I was too
distracted to hear—

Black lipstick!

Gulp.

Suddenly my memory was jogged. All the awful
things I said about her came flooding back to me. Not
just about her mosquito bites and black lipstick, but
also about the fact that she frightened me and that she
was the only kid in any of my classes whose house I
wouldn't go to even if I were invited.

No wonder she'd been looking for me. She wanted
to give me what for.

I decided to keep climbing the stairs and act like I
didn't hear her.

"Raisin?" she called out again.

"What? I made a mistake! I'm sorry! If you want to
take a shot at me, go ahead, but I'll have you know I'm
freakishly strong!"

Now I think it was me who frightened her.

"Why would I want to take a shot at you? I think
you're awesome," she said.

"You do?" I asked.

"That's what I've been trying to tell you."

It's true, that *is* what she'd been trying to tell me. I

don't know why I was making it so difficult for her to speak her truth.

"But what about all those things I said about you? They weren't exactly nice."

"I don't like nice. Nice is for the masses. I much prefer alienation. You seem to as well."

I wanted to tell her that I preferred wild popularity. But it seemed like the wrong time to quibble over words.

"All my friends think you're awesome too," she said, waving her hand past a whole bunch of kids.

Even dressed within the limits of the school code, they were outfitted to scare. Their shirts were unbuttoned to reveal ripped T-shirts and strange body jewelry. Their hair was dyed every color of the rainbow. They had safety pins poking through any place you could imagine. And possibly places you couldn't. Even the boys' ties were menacing—patterned with deadly snakes or skulls and crossbones.

Out of all of them, the only one I recognized was the guy with green hair, who's running against Fiona. His name is Roman and today he was wearing a dog leash around his neck—not just the collar, mind you, the whole leash.

"So Raisin, would you like to join my 'zine? We're looking for kids with strong points of view," Kim said.

I know beggars can't be choosers. But I had to think it over. For one thing, I'm not really sure what a point of view is. And for another, if I wrote for her e-zine, I'd have to spend time with those kids. And in case I haven't been clear, they frightened me.

But maybe I wasn't being honest with myself. It's easy to say that they frighten me. That makes *them* the freaks. But maybe what I really felt was intimidated. They just seemed so much cooler than me. As if they listen to bands with words like *death, destruction,* and *demonic* in the title. And throw pianos out of hotel windows. Whereas *I* listen to bands with the words *Britney Spears* in the title and never break my eight o'clock curfew without calling first.

But in everyone's life, there comes a time to take a walk on the wild side.

"Sure, Kim, I'd love to. What's it called?"

"CoolerThanYou," she answered.

Just what I needed to hear. They might as well have named it *AllMyFearsConfirmed.*

"Great, and when's the next meeting?"

"Tomorrow. My basement. Four o'clock. Here's the address."

She wrote down the information on a slip of paper and handed it to me. At the top of the page was written *Lynn Weingarten's house.*

"Is Lynn your sister?" I asked.

"No," she answered. "That's my name, Lynn."

"It is?" I asked, feeling pretty stupid. "But I keep calling you Kim. Doesn't that bother you?"

"Not really. As long as I know my name, what difference does it make if other people do?" Lynn asked.

An interesting way to look at things, I suppose. But for the record, if she ever decides that knowing her own name isn't important, I might have to disagree with her.

PS—CJ started a new cartoon today. I wonder if that means something?

PPS—Only six days until the election. If Fiona murders me, I wonder if my new friends will still like me.

PPSS—I wish I could convince them all to vote for Fiona to increase her chances. But with Roman running, it seems pretty unlikely.

Fiona must win. Fiona must win.

Comments:

Logged in at 8:03 PM, EST

<u>PiaBallerina</u>: I bet your new friends will like you no matter what Fiona does.

Logged in at 8:11 PM, EST

<u>kweenclaudia</u>: they sound smelly.

Logged in at 8:14 PM, EST

<u>PiaBallerina</u>: Claudia!

Logged in at 8:17 PM, EST

<u>kweenclaudia</u>: i'm sorry. i meant, smelly but nice!

Thursday, November 4

6:36 PM, EST

Hello Kitties!

Frightening is fun for the whole family!

But before I go into any further detail, allow me to begin by saying that I was the best-dressed person at the meeting today. In all fairness, there wasn't much competition. Those kids seem to shop at the bottom of their local Dumpsters. Still, it's nice to feel special.

Where was I? Right, the meeting . . .

I was expecting Lynn's house to be a little spooky. But it was really nice. The basement especially. The chairs were very modern, like they came out of *The Jetsons* or something, and there was a giant white throw rug. She even served a normal snack of soda and chips. I must say, I was half expecting her to serve fresh blood and rat tails.

Roman reviewed the 'zine submission guidelines. They are as follows:

1. Dude, write about whatever you want. I'm not your mother.

2. Don't glorify The Man.

Everyone seemed to know who The Man was except for me.

"You mean Principal Sloan?" I asked.

"Principal Sloan, Vice Principal Gray, your parents . . ."

I was lost.

"My parents? But what if your mom's not a man? Take my mom, for instance. She's a woman."

"That's okay. The Man is anyone who tries to keep the rest of us down. Your mom, the school nurse, Fiona and her cohorts . . ."

Fiona? What was he talking about? I continued to be lost.

"Fiona? What are you talking about? I continue to be lost!" I said.

A quiet roar overtook Lynn's basement. There was name-calling. Gesticulating. Chest thumping.

I sensed some anger.

"Raisin," Roman began as he wiped his nose with his hand, "I'm not about telling people what to think. It's not who I am. But you are so wrong about Fiona Small. She *is* The Man. She thinks she's better than everyone else. She doesn't like anyone who's different. And she'll step over anyone who tries to get in her way. That's why I'm running against her in the election."

"So you're still pretty set on that, are ya?" I asked.

"Absolutely," he said.

Oh, well. It was worth a shot.

5:41 PM, EST

No one's home. I'm so excited about my new friends at the 'zine, and I have no one to tell. Not even Jeremy. If I called him, he'd just tell me to find someone who doesn't suffer from chronic loudyitis, or give macadamia nuts as gifts, or have friends who sweat, and see if that person cares. And he'd be totally justified.

I'm taking Countess for a walk.

5:43 PM, EST

Did you guys catch that? I just decided to take Countess for a walk completely of my own volition.

This Jeremy thing must really have me down.

6:43 PM, EST

Just came back from my walk. Countess barked his head off when we passed Giselle's. They just got in their holiday collection, which is very pink and glittery. That must have been what got him so excited. I'd have barked my head off too, but I'm in enough trouble as it is. Then again, the 'zine people would probably love me for barking. It's so alienating.

I gave Countess some time to admire the fabulosity and tried to move him along. He refused. His paws were dug firmly into the ground and he wasn't leaving. As gorgeous as the outfits were, he could never pull any of them off. It's sad, really. Samantha's really got him believing he's a girl.

I tugged a bit more at his leash, but it didn't help.

"Countess, what do you want?"

He continued barking, his eyes fixed on the Red Leather Bag. Yes, that's correct. Gisselle's just got a shipment of the very red leather bags with pink monograms preferred by Fiona and her friends. I could tell he wanted me to have that bag. It makes sense. Dogs are really sensitive to their human's needs. So I tied him to a lamppost and bought the bag with my saved-up allowance.

When I came out of the store, his tongue was hanging from his mouth and he was furiously wagging his tail. I haven't seen him so happy since the night Horace brought home a shank bone from one of his dinners.

So now I have the bag. I do still love it even though it didn't come from Fiona.

On the walk home, I decided that my first "piece" (ha! I'm so fancy, I'm writing a "piece") for the 'zine would be about Jeremy. And how great he is.

Then maybe he'll forgive me.

PS—Fiona must win the election.

Fiona must win the election.

Comments:

Logged in at 7:36 PM, EST

PiaBallerina: Rae-rae, I'm sure Fiona will win, but even if she doesn't, what can she do to hurt you now? You're an alterna-girl now, with alterna-friends.

Logged in at 7:49 PM, EST

kweenclaudia: lol! you got your bag from a male dog dressed as a girl instead of a girl who's really the man. or something clever like that . . . i'm having trouble concentrating. mailbox boy—clint—got his nose pierced for real. i think i might like him again!

Friday, November 5

Greetings, Kitty Cats,

Pi—you're so right! Fiona can't hurt me now. But let's hold off on referring to me as an alterna-person just yet. I like them. They like me. But their fashion sense is for the birds. Hopefully we can all come to some kind of agreement.

I finished my piece ("piece!" ha!) on Jeremy. It's called "Jeremy Craine, Profile in Courage." I can't wait till it's posted so he can read it.

PS—CJ switched from the Armani bag to a Banana Republic bag. . . . Now I'm really worried.

Comments:

Logged in at 8:42 PM, EST

<u>PiaBallerina</u>: But didn't you say his other bag was falling apart? I bet he didn't read the blog. If he doesn't talk to anyone, how could he have found out about it?

Logged in at 8:47 PM, EST

<u>kweenclaudia</u>: p's right. unless that cartoon he's always working on came to life and told him, he probably has no way of knowing.

Monday, November 8

7:03 AM, EST

Kittyliciousness,

I hope you guys are right. . . .

For the sake of compromise, I tried to incorporate a little alt into my look today. Ripped fishnets and smart monogrammed bags just don't go together. So I wore my favorite jeans and a smart black turtleneck instead. My new friends will just have to love me for who I am. Not for who I'm trying to be.

12:40 PM, EST

Still figuring out who I'm trying to be. Toward that end, I left my new bag in my locker during lunchtime. In the long run, it was a better choice. For me and for the bag.

I passed Jeremy on the lunch line. He didn't even say hi to me. He was still eating the cottage cheese, though. Why should I be surprised? Without me in his life, who's he got to look after his better interests?

I brought my lunch to the back stairwell, where Lynn and Roman and all their friends now eat. Imagine that! My little ol' stairwell is now an underground hot spot. I started a trend!

BTW—Lynn eats the tuna casserole. She must be trying to alienate herself.

4:54 PM, EST

I still have CJ under close observation. He gives no clear indication as to whether he's read the blog. Which is better than throwing tampons at my head. But not as good as professing his undying love to me.

Comments:

Logged in at 7:07 PM, EST

<u>kweenclaudia</u>: **all this talk about tuna casserole has made me want to try it.**

8:53 PM, EST

I almost forgot to mention—I submitted my piece about Jeremy today. I can't wait till he reads it!

Tuesday, November 9

12:03 PM, EST

Kittens,

Today was election day. Just to be on the safe side, I voted for Fiona four times. Once after each class and once during homeroom. I might not need her as a friend anymore, but I still need her not to cause me bodily harm.

Besides, it was so easy! The election's done by secret ballot and there was a different teacher manning the ballot box each period. No one seemed to notice.

4:56 PM, EST

Fiona won.

They announced it over the loudspeaker during last period, which I happen to have with Roman. He didn't look too happy when I accidentally yelled out, "Yippee!"

I hope he's not too upset about losing. He'd definitely make the better president.

Comments:

Logged in at 7:37 PM, EST

<u>PiaBallerina</u>: I knew Fiona would win. That's how it is with the popular kids. They always manage to come out on top.

Logged in at 7:46 PM, EST

<u>kweenclaudia</u>: **i think i'm starting to have a crush on roman.**

Wednesday, November 10

4:57 PM, EST

Felines,

No word from Jeremy yet.

Thursday, November 11

5:36 PM, EST

KittyClaudia and KittyPia,

I passed Jeremy seventeen times today and he didn't say a word. Seventeen times!

I don't think he even reads *CoolerThanYou*. He's probably never heard of *CoolerThanYou*. I'd never heard of *CoolerThanYou* before Lynn came along. *CoolerThanYou* is too cool for the likes of me and Jeremy. *CoolerThanYou* is so cool, it's too cool for anyone to actually read.

What was I thinking?

Enough of this alt business. I'm going mainstream. I'm going to submit the piece to the school newspaper. I bet Jeremy reads that. It's so easy too. All I have to do is e-mail it in.

I'm going to do that right now.

Friday, November 12

___

6:57 PM, EST

Catwomen,

You'll never guess who just called me.

Fiona!

Turns out she's the human interest editor of the school newspaper. Class president, editor, being The Man—it amazes me how she fits it all in.

It was so strange to hear her voice.

"I was just calling to see if you had a picture of Jeremy that I could print alongside the article."

"Who is this?"

"It's Fiona."

"But you hate me. Why are you calling?" I asked.

"Because I'm the editor of the school newspaper. Didn't you know? Besides, I think you actually helped me win the election. People like me more after reading your blog. That conversation we had in the bathroom kind of showed off my sensitive side."

Figures that Fiona would be the one person to benefit from my blog.

"But weren't your friends mad at you for saying that they didn't understand?" I asked. I'd been feeling so guilty about that.

"At first, a little. But we talked about it, and now

they do understand. In the end it was kinda good."

"Well, I'm glad it worked out . . ." I said.

There was a short pause. I think I was waiting for her to say she missed me, or that life wasn't the same without me, or that she'd like to have me over for a mud pack some time.

"So, send me that picture, okay?" she said.

"Okay, Fiona . . ." I said. And that was that.

The only picture I have of Jeremy is from my mom's wedding. It's of the two of us dancing. I can't even cut myself out of it because then it'll just be a picture of one-half of Jeremy's face.

This must be a test. To see how far I'll go to earn Jeremy's forgiveness. Well, you know what? I can pass this test. Let everyone think what they want when they see a picture of Jeremy and me slow dancing in formal wear. I don't care.

I'll do whatever it takes to win him back.

Comments:

Logged in at 8:03 PM, EST

PiaBallerina: I have a good feeling about this, Rae.

Logged in at 8:10 PM, EST

kweenclaudia: i hope p's right, for goodness sake. i'd really like to get on with this whole jeremy thing. . . .

Sunday, November 14

8:56 PM, EST

Dearest Kitties,

I sent Fiona the jpeg of me and Jeremy at the wedding. At least I like the dress I'm wearing. It's an off-the-shoulders gown made of periwinkle blue satin with a lace bodice.

Today Lynn and I went to hear Roman's band practice. They're called Rodenticide and they're really good.

I think.

"Tight," as Lynn kept saying.

One thing I know is that they're very loud. And that I stuck out like a sore thumb in my lavender camisole and matching cardigan ensemble. I probably shouldn't have worn it. But I couldn't stop myself.

Some people like to look alienating and frightening.

Others like to look pretty.

After practice I went to dinner with my family. It was Horace's birthday. I was glad because now *he* had to wear the Krispy Kreme birthday crown. He didn't seem to mind it as much as I did.

Before the cake came, he made a toast:

"To my lovely wife, Patricia, and daughters, Samantha, Raisin, and Lola. Thank you for making this the best year of my life."

I wish I could say his corny toast gave me that potato-salad feeling in the back of my throat. But between you and me, I didn't really mind it too much. And if it weren't for the piece of spinach stuck in between his two front teeth when he made the toast, I might not have minded it at all.

Just as I was wondering if my mom minded the spinach, she raised her glass to make a toast as well. I've never been a huge fan of my mother's toasts. After all, the last one she made brought about one of the worst events in history. But this one gave me one of those warm and tingly feelings all over.

"To my wonderful husband, Horace, and my daughters, Sam, Raisin, and Lola, thank you for making this the best year of *my* life."

I mean, I know it's the same toast Horace made, but I liked it more coming from her. Maybe it's because she's prettier than he is.

After my mom's toast, Samantha gave me one of those little squeezes again. It made me feel so good, I tried giving one to Lola. Mine was a little too hard, though. It made Lola yelp. I've got to ask Sam what her secret is.

I guess my family isn't all that bad. It's comforting to know that if I ever lose all my friends again, I could always become one of those kids who *enjoys* hanging out with her relatives. Who isn't embarrassed to be seen at Chuck E. Cheese with her parents and younger siblings and who says things like, "My mom is my best friend," and, "Prom, shmom, I went to the library with my stepdad last night and we found a really great book about insects and their effect on the square root of nine."

Comments:

Logged in at 9:37 PM, EST

<u>kweenclaudia</u>: that's kinda touching.

Logged in at 9:43 PM, EST

<u>PiaBallerina</u>: What's going on, Claudia?

Logged in at 9:45 PM, EST

<u>kweenclaudia</u>: what makes you think something's going on?

Logged in at 9:50 PM, EST

<u>PiaBallerina</u>: You're being all nice and sweet. And not all jokey. It's not really like you.

Logged in at 9:51 PM, EST

<u>kweenclaudia</u>: okay, okay, you got me. i kissed Mailbox Boy!

Monday, November 15

7:03 AM, EST

Kitties,

Claudia, that's so great! I hope this doesn't mean you're going to be nice *all* the time from now on. You already tried that once, and I'm not sure I liked it.

7:14 PM, EST

Oh, the leaves are changing, the air is getting crisper, Claudia's got a sexy new boyfriend, and all is right with the world again!

There's still hope for me and CJ. . . .

Today there was a 'zine meeting at Lynn's, and who should show up but Mr. Gorgeous himself. He's our new illustrator.

I was so mortified, I almost left. I still didn't know whether he read the blog. What if he and I had to work together? I mean, I wasn't so sure how that could work, seeing as he doesn't really like to speak, but still, what if?

Turns out, we did have to work together.

"Raisin, I want you to work with CJ. Come up with a caption for the cartoon he's drawing," Lynn said.

Had she taken leave of her senses? I wondered.

I grabbed her by the elbow and led her into a corner.

"But I can't work with him. What if he read the blog? It's too embarrassing!"

"But you *have* to work with him. I picked you because you're funny. Besides, I bet he didn't read the blog. He probably doesn't even know about it," she said, sounding a little impatient.

I didn't want to disappoint her. So I went to her bathroom to collect myself. It's a good thing too because when I looked in the mirror, my hair was all out of whack. You know how you leave the house thinking you look gorgeous and then when you check yourself out later in the day, you look like Gollum from *Lord of the Rings*? I couldn't have CJ see me like this.

I went back to the meeting and CJ was drawing away like he was under one of his weird spells.

I looked at the drawings and racked my brain for caption ideas. But I was too distracted to concentrate. I had to get it over with. I just had to ask.

"Hey, CJ—have you heard about Mervis?"

"Huh?" he said, looking at me like I was a visitor from outer space.

"*Mervis?* Does the name *Mervis* mean anything to you at all?" I asked, slowly enunciating the name Mervis for emphasis.

He gave me another freaky look. "Who's Mervis?" he asked, and went back to his work.

There's still hope! CJ didn't read the blog! He doesn't know about my desperate attempts to make friends. Or that I live in a loony bin. Or that I once made out with a textbook! Or about my insane love for him.

He also doesn't seem to have much of a problem speaking to me. He said three whole words to me. Eleven, including last time!

But most of all, he doesn't know who Mervis is.

He may not know who I am either, but I can live with that for now.

Tuesday, November 16

4:33 PM, EST

Kitty Cats,

The school paper came out today. Sparkles was the first to tell me about it. Of course.

He was waiting for me in front of my locker when I got to school, with the paper opened to my piece. It was weird to see that picture of myself in an actual newspaper.

"Merve," he said. (For some reason, I allow him to call me that. But *only* him, Claud . . .) "You know I love you, but this prom rag you've got on isn't working for you at all. Next time I'd go for something a little more sophisticated. Maybe a pants suit . . ."

Then I saw Hailey, Madison, and Bliss during homeroom.

"Nice piece, Raisin. If you wrote something like that about us, we might consider forgiving you," Hailey said. Bliss and Madison just broke out into laughter.

Roger Morris got behind me on the lunch line. "Ya done good, Raisin," he said, towering over me. I swear that kid gets bigger every day.

Why has everyone read the piece except for Jeremy? Where's he been? I wonder if he hated it and now he's avoiding me.

6:56 PM, EST

Still haven't heard from Jeremy. Now I'm really worried. What if I made things worse?

7:15 PM, EST

I called Jeremy's house. When he answered, I hung up.

7:20 PM, EST

I can't remember if he has caller ID or not.

7:32 PM, EST

If he's home, why hasn't he called me? Why isn't he showering me with gratitude?

7:37 PM, EST

?!

9:06 PM, EST

I got tired of sitting around and waiting for Jeremy to thank me, so I went to his house to speed things up.

"I was about to call you. I just got back from visiting my grandmother. Thanks so much for writing that stuff about me. It was really sweet," he said.

"So you liked it?" I asked.

"Yeah, mostly," he said as he took a seat on his front stoop.

"Mostly? Why? What didn't you like? Did you feel like it was braggy? Because it doesn't count as braggy if you're not the one who's saying the braggy things."

"I didn't feel like it was braggy," he said. "I feel like it was lie-y."

He had a point. There was one or two things that I made up.

Maybe I should show it to you guys so you can see for yourself:

An Open Letter to the Public About Jeremy Craine

Dear Public,

As some of you might have heard, recently a secret blog was discovered and circulated through the seventh grade. As a result of this unfortunate episode, a girl's secrets were revealed. She was called some nasty names. She lost some friends. She was utterly humiliated. My heart goes out to this girl, whoever she is.

But what happened to the girl wasn't the worst outcome of this event. The worst outcome was that there were some unkind words written in the blog about a boy named Jeremy Craine. They weren't only unkind. They were also completely untrue. The girl who wrote them must be a complete dodo-head. Again, my heart goes out to her, whoever she is.

Jeremy Craine is not someone who deserves unkind words. Jeremy Craine is someone who deserves to be honored. He's smart, funny, and fun to be with. He's a great shopper, gift-giver, soccer teacher, and poster-maker. He can also do this really neat trick where he turns his eyelids inside out.

But he's so much more.

Jeremy Craine is very quick—he once caught a mugger red-handed. Jeremy Craine is a brilliant prank caller—he once appeared on the cable TV show *Cranked!* Jeremy Craine is very brave—he once saved a girl who fell down a well. He's also very modest. He'd never mention these things himself.

But none of these qualities, though all true, are what make Jeremy so unique. What makes Jeremy so unique is that he is the truest, most loyal, most devoted friend a person can have. He always puts others first. And himself last. A friend of Jeremy's is a lucky person indeed.

Incidentally, he's also very hot. If you've ever thought of going out with him, or even if you haven't, now would be a good time to step up to the plate.

Thank you for your time,

Raisin Rodriguez

(Pretty flattering, don't you guys agree?)

"I don't think of it as lying," I told him. "I think of it more as truth stretching. Maybe you didn't catch a mugger, but you did catch a nose picker, which is also an offense. And maybe you weren't on *Cranked!,* but if you keep coming up with funny ideas for prank calls, you could be. And maybe you didn't save a little girl who fell down a well, but you did kind of save me. You befriended me when no one else would. You helped me with soccer and the posters. You warned me about the blog. You . . . looked out for me when I had no one." I got a little teary at that last part.

"That's nice, I guess. . . . But it makes me wonder if the real me is interesting enough for you," he said.

"The real you is more than interesting enough for

me. It just might not be interesting enough for the school paper. So I added some extra stuff to make sure the piece got printed," I began as my nose started to run.

"Oh, Raisin, you'll never change," he said as he handed me a tissue from his pants' pocket.

Neither will he. He's still got that awful loudyitis.

Then I blew my nose. It made a honking noise, which embarrassed me until Jeremy started cracking up, which made me realize how funny it was. When we stopped laughing, I still had one more question to ask him.

"What about Fiona? I put in the part about you being hot mostly for her benefit."

"I could never go out with her," he said.

"Why not?"

"Because I don't think she's so nice. Hearing all that stuff about her from the blog made me realize that the only person she really cares about is Fiona."

"Wow," I said. "You're a really good person." Then I hugged him.

I'm so lucky that I met him—and that he forgave me. And I'm really glad that I'm making friends with Lynn, and Roman, and all the 'zine people. I mean, don't get me wrong, they're not you guys. No one could ever be. But it's nice to have them in my life.

I bet that's how Gordo felt about his new friends. Ioiu'p 9 popopoiooiljdkjkajdlkajlkjsdlkjpoieu poupouu-jlkjdfhkjashf;kjhkajhfo/9ppoUgggh!! Guess who? Kjlkjl kjljhklkj owio[iim9iwoioidjlkjlkjlkjlkjlkjlkjlkjljljlkjlkjljljl I better go.

Lola's wiping her nose on my comforter!

PS—You know how they tell you to put toothpaste on your zits to make them go away? It really works!

PPS—Paste. Not gel!